Liar, Liar

Alan McMonagle

Wordsonthestreet

First published 2008 by
Wordsonthestreet
Six San Antonio Park, Salthill, Galway, Ireland
Web: www.wordsonthestreet.com
Email: publisher@wordsonthestreet.com

A catalogue record for this book is available from the British Library.

ISBN   0-9552604-5-0
            978-0-9552604-5-2

Cover Design: Wordsonthestreet
Layout and typesetting: Wordsonthestreet
Printed and bound in the UK

Liar, Liar

Acknowledgements

Acknowledgment is due to the editors of the following magazines where some of these stories first appeared:

Crannóg Magazine
   (*My Good Lady, The Man who is afraid of Cows, Lap Dancing*).
West47 online and The Cúirt Annual
   (*Late Night Coffee, Billabong* and *Sun Showers*).
WOW!
   (*Saturday Night at the Movies*).
The Stinging Fly
   (*The Worst Person In Ireland*).
Southword
   (*The Wake, Liar, Liar*).
Pindeldyboz
   (*Love Hearts*).
Windows Publications *Authors & Artists Introduction Series*
   (*The Lake Isle*).

The quote on page 38
... there is no sublime; only the shining of the amnion's tatters
is from the poem *Oatmeal* by Galway Kinnell.

for fionnuala

Contents

The Wake

Now that he was dead and safely buried well out of harm's way, everyone thought the Briar Martin was a great fellow.

He was full of brains. He had the soul of a poet. He knew everything there was to know about cars. He was a marvellous observer. He was a personal friend of fish.

All this upset me no end.

'Why didn't they tell him all this when he was alive and well, making all our lives a misery?' I asked.

'Because you can't have your cake and eat it,' said my grandfather.

The Briar Martin was my mother's brother, my uncle. He was the black sheep of the family. He never married, never had a career, never had a good thing to say, never smiled – at least not in public. He didn't even own a mobile phone and this signified to everyone that he really wanted nothing to do with the world. His idea of a good time was to rest his elbows on the bar counter, prop his chin in his hands, frown and stare into the black abyss of his glass. He could do this for hours on end. Finally, he might shift in his stool, emit a long grunt, raise his glass and drink deep. His glass was always half full when he ordered another. Or half empty, which everyone assumed was the way he looked at the glass. It was part of his un-cheery outlook, they said. That man was contrary before there were reasons to be contrary, they also said and nodded wisely. Everyone assumed he was an unhappy man.

My mother seemed upset that her brother was dead. But she had another one. One who was married, who had a career, had lots of good things to say and who never stopped smiling – at least not in public. In actual fact, he had two careers, and a car for each of them. He also owned two mobile phones. Which, in a way, made up for the black sheep. His name was Pete.

At the wake for the Briar Martin, Pete spoke to me like a teacher or one of those guys on the radio who always interrupt the songs they play to tell us how good they are. He provided ideas on how to go about tackling the future. Could I rely on my brains, he wondered. Become a solicitor and the owner of a dry cleaning business, he suggested. Don't pay tax at source, he warned. As he spoke, his voice moved up and down and every sentence sounded like it was a question. The first opportunity I got, I ran away from him. Besides, I was interested in finding out more things about the dead man.

Everyone called him the Briar Martin. Including me and my mother and my grandfather. So too lots of long lost cousins who arrived steadily from New Zealand and Canada and said they couldn't recognise the place. Except Pete. Pete didn't call him anything as his repeated attempts to save his brother from himself had gone unacknowledged. They hadn't spoken together for a long time. But it had no affect on Pete's smiling face, or on the Briar Martin's bleak outlook. So perhaps it's true that certain things are best left alone. And also that people don't say what they're thinking.

At the wake, everyone scattered themselves about the room, grabbed sandwiches and talked about the cost of living and climate change. Now and then, they considered the dead man's life. They spoke in low huddles but I could hear everything because in those days my mother was keeping me alive with a diet of turnips, and when I tried to tell her they made me feel ill, she placed her hands on her hips and said *eat your turnips or you'll go deaf.* It was something she had to tell me many times. *I can't seem to get through to you* was another thing she often said. So if I wanted to stay alive, let alone not go deaf, I had to eat her lumpy turnips. Otherwise I would perish obscurely like the Briar Martin. It was a difficult choice but, as I chewed the yellow mush, I did notice that my hearing improved remarkably. In fact, though I was still small, I was already at the stage where I could hear the things people were thinking about. So I continued to eat turnips in the hope that I would be able to hear the Briar Martin's opinions on all this royal talk about him – now that he was absent and powerless to disagree.

Because it seemed that everyone was involved in a case of mistaken identity. As far as I could make out, they were talking about a completely different person. I scanned the room to make sure I was attending the correct celebration. I saw my mother, her brother and my grandfather. They were in conversation with people who tripped over themselves to say a great compliment about the dead man – the deceased, they called him. They continued to say only proper and appropriate things. And, concerning my no-good miserable unacknowledging black sheep uncle they even volunteered sympathetic reasons for his anguish.

'Perhaps there was a deep tragedy in his past that prevented him getting on with his life.'

'Maybe he was bitter over an unrequited affair of romance.'

'His morbidity was down to the unfulfilled promise of youth.'

If only he was alive to hear this, I kept saying to myself. He'd set them straight on a few things.

On one thing they were unanimous: he would be missed.

'So why are they saying they miss him?' I asked my grandfather.

'Because it's the truth,' he replied.

'But they're telling lies about him. Saying he could fix cars and compose poems and was sensitive like the fish. He was a miserable sod and well they know. They're as bad as my mother.'

'What has your mother done to you?'

'She makes me eat turnips. She doesn't even know how to cook them properly. They taste like rocks. Only worse. She says they're good for me and that's a lie.'

'If your mother says you must eat turnips, eat them. You'll thank her for it one day.'

'I'll thank her on the day I get a decent meal,' I said. 'A burger and some chips. And onion rings. She is contributing to my distress.'

'Don't distress yourself too much, Kevin. Your uncle is at peace.'

'So why talk about him like that? Make him out to be a different person?'

'Because there is something worse than talking about someone, no matter what is said,' said my grandfather.

'What's that?' I asked.

'Forgetting,' he replied.

During this confusing conversation my mother sauntered over. Concerning the progress of her brother's farewell she had probably heard my objections. But I was too worried to notice that she was speaking to me. And then shouting.

'Earth calling Kevin. Come in Kevin. AM I TALKING TO MYSELF?'

She was always saying things like that to me. *Knock, knock, is there anyone home? Listen carefully, I'm not going to say this again.* But she always did and I couldn't stop giggling. This made things between us worse. *What does it take to get through to you? I don't know why you were given ears. Are you listening to me Kevin Prendergast?*

She must have had little faith in her turnips, I supposed. Not that I blamed her. But there was not a thing wrong with my ears. It was true I had an alarming pain in the left one when I was very small. I cried and cried and my mother marched me to the doctor and he forced a Hoover inside my head which removed two large waxy black lumps. Then I was given a squirt-bottle of drops and the doctor spoke with my mother. It was shortly after that she started me on the turnips, and my ears announced themselves in the most annoying ways. At night, I could hear water dripping from a faulty tap; the ticking of a distant clock; the pitter-patter of ghosts. Meanwhile, the drops were doing their bit. My ears grew and grew out of the side of my head like aeroplane wings. If I ran fast enough I was sure to take off. If someone took a notion, they could have lifted me up like the winning trophy. So why was my mother so obsessed? If anything, she should have been trying to take my attention away from these freaky growths. And why did she call me by my full name as though I was a complete and utter stranger to her?

All these questions I had no idea how to answer. I returned to my listening and paid attention to three wise-looking men with glasses of whiskey. They were talking but not to each other. They were talking about the Briar Martin and they took turns to say something to the wall they were leaning against.

'He was one of those people with no ambition. No get up and go. No drive. Where I come from, we call those people space-wasters.'

'His attitude was wrong. I once heard him mutter *when life ends death ends.* Life was wasted on him.'

'He was born under a pessimistic sign, but I'll say this for him - he was a good man to borrow money off, because he never expected to get it back.'

This is more like it, I said to myself. There are still some people who try to tell the truth. These outpourings were much closer to the heart of the matter. It hit me that if everyone was left alone to themselves, really thinking, imagine all the good stuff I could find out. Whiskey was obviously part of it as well.

So I hunted down some lonely people who had turned to

drink, and the truly awful things they had to say about the dead man brought an enormous smile to my face. They were mighty things and I hoped they would think similarly of me when my time came. I said as much to my grandfather.

'Somehow, I think things will be different for you,' he said. 'And you'll outlive us all.'

'Oh don't say things like that grandfather,' I replied, with a hint of panic in my voice. 'It won't be the same with you lot not around to tell lies about me as I pass on to a higher plane.'

'Why are you so obsessed with old men and dying?' my grandfather asked me.

'It's the way I am,' I replied. 'Deep down I am a very troubled person. You could say I am a younger version of the Briar Martin.'

'Do you want to be unhappy?' he asked.

'Of course not, but I can't alter my chromosomes.'

'Your what?'

'I heard them say that the Briar Martin inherited a bad set of chromosomes. I could have as well.'

'And what does your mother think of this chromosome business?'

'Mother definitely has a bad set. She's not able to get through to me. She has started putting rocks in my stew. She says it's for my own good.'

My grandfather was laughing now. It was a gentle laugh but it made him sound as if he was out of breath. I thought it was no way to behave on the day of the Briar Martin's wake.

'You don't know what it's like grandfather,' I pleaded. 'Some of my troubles go so deep a submarine wouldn't find them.'

But my yearning fell on another pair of deaf ears. He was also bending over and his face was reddening from all the laughter. A ropey vein throbbed out of his neck and blue wriggly strands appeared on his nose.

'This isn't a laughing matter, grandfather,' I said as sternly as possible.

'No, no it isn't. But you shouldn't take things to heart so much.'

That was the last straw as far as I was concerned. I was now in official dispute with everyone close to me. My rock-baking mother. Her career-collecting brother. And now my laughing grandfather. None of these people seemed prepared to take my anxieties seriously. What was the point in being alive if I couldn't take things to heart? I had to get this through to them and I saw only one other course of action left for me to take.

Just before the fiddle players started pulling their bows of woe and regret, I announced my intentions to go on hunger strike.

And I went outside.

I sat on the garden wall, rested my chin in my hands and tried to frown the way I had seen the Briar Martin do it on one of the last times I had seen him. It was during an especially difficult time for my mother to get through to me. I couldn't bear to listen to anything she tried to say to me and one afternoon I escaped from the house and followed the Briar Martin into the pub. It was my first time in the pub. It was small and narrow, with a low ceiling and no windows. My uncle was the only other person there. He recognised me and he gestured to a stool beside him. He put a mineral in front of me and it was quiet for a long time. The two of us just sat there and I enjoyed the silence. 'Do you know why I like this place so much?' he said to me after an age. 'There is no coverage for mobile phones.' Then he chuckled away to himself.

Eventually, my mother tried to tease me out of my strike. She came to me with a bowl of mush and I told her what I thought of her cooking. Her brother appeared with his up and down voice and I added not-talking to my strike. Then they sent out my grandfather.

He sat down on the low wall and didn't say a thing. I soon became fed up with all this quiet between us.

'Are you not talking either?' I asked him.

'It seems you and I have something in common,' he said. 'When I was in the army they fed us turnips. It was during The Emergency. Don't ask me about The Emergency because I haven't got all day to put you in a good mood. But you're right about one thing. I have just tasted your mother's cooking. These turnips need something.'

Later, after everyone had eaten all the sandwiches and drank the whiskey and wobbled off to stare longingly at the Briar Martin's empty bar stool, grandfather showed us how to make an onion-gravy that soaked up every single piece of turnip on the plate. Straightaway they tasted better and that night I heard the dead whispering jokes to each other.

In time, many more unhappy uncles and aunts came out of the woodwork to be buried. I returned from my own quest for happiness and spent a few days with my mother and my uncle Pete who, by then, had accumulated five careers, five cars, a cottage on the island of Cyprus, a valuable portfolio of mobile phones and three spoilt brats via a second wife. It's best not to mention his voice.

And I developed a genuine liking for turnips, a development which has aided beyond measure my joust with life, as I can hear what people are saying in Africa and Ecuador and I listen to what everyone thinks and I know parts of the answers to questions before I even ask them. So no one is fooling me.

I even rang my mother and thanked her – just like grandfather said I would. I could hear him laughing as well, wherever he was, and his gentle wheezing reminded me of youthful time spent in his company searching for the roots of my unhappiness. Unforgotten time. And it occurs to me that, maybe, I hadn't been as troubled as I thought I was.

Love Hearts

t always rains on Juliet's side of the road. The shoes she likes never come in her size. The pay rise promised to her is postponed yet again. The friend she wants to meet has made other plans. 'Let me out of this world,' she screeches, when her work phone goes off at four o'clock in the morning. Her umbrella never stands a chance.

Nor is solace to be found in cyberspace. Worms frequently attack her e-mail. Six times in the past year, hackers have taken her Visa numbers. Last Wednesday, she Googled her name and discovered that very night she was to be executed by lethal injection at a correctional facility in Texas.

Cycling home from work in the rain, I often receive a text message: *Play the Lotto - You are luckier than me.* When she finally gets home herself, her drenched expression says it all: *Life is disappointing.* For some reason, she puts me in mind of the little boy let down by his Christmas trip to Lapland because Rudolph didn't have a red nose and throwing snowballs was forbidden.

Since Juliet made friends with misfortune we have been

going to bed early. There is never anything on television. We've listened to all our CDs. Some time ago, we threw out our board games. We may as well be in bed as anywhere, we concluded, raising our eyebrows at each other.

In the bedroom, we draw the curtains, slide inside the covers and turn on our bedside lamps. Juliet watches a moth dance in the glow, absentmindedly files her nails, wishes awful things upon her boss. From time to time she swears tomorrow is her last day. I pull out my locker drawer, flick through my collection of bookmarks, peek inside my Credit Union book to remind myself I can get through tomorrow. From time to time I contribute gruesome methods to seeing off Juliet's boss.

Occasionally I read to Juliet. Occasionally she reads to me. I read from Edgar Allen Poe's *Tales of Mystery and Imagination*. Juliet reads from *1,001 Things To Do Before You Die*. I find Juliet's pre-death experiences utterly terrifying. She considers my rendering of Edgar Allen neither mysterious nor imaginative. So we put down our books and pop a Love Heart.

'What does yours say?' Juliet asks.

'Hug me,' I say.

'Fat chance,' she replies, showing hers.

We started popping Love Hearts last Halloween, just after we moved into our new home. Lots of others had moved out this way too, and Juliet bought a bumper bag of treats for the Halloween children. But on the night, they didn't knock on our door.

We were a little disappointed, as we had prepared ourselves for a long night of fun. Right inside our front door we placed two kitchen chairs. And between the chairs rested a large fruit bowl, into which were heaped the contents from the bumper bag of goodies. To ensure a level of comfort throughout the night ahead, Juliet even puffed up a pillow and placed it on her chair. While in the hallway, I fitted an evil-green light bulb and hung a Frankenstein skeleton to promote the seasonal mood.

Just after dark we sat into the chairs and waited for the first callers. We were sure it was just a matter of moments away. We could hear their giddy footsteps taking them from door to door, their trick-or-treat homilies, their shadowy rustlings. But, when our turn came, the children skipped silently across our driveway.

Contributing to our disappointment was the entertainment we had missed out on. I'm quite keen on the masks and scary death make-up the children put on. Juliet had been looking forward to a haphazard song, a bungled trick, a budding witch's cautionary tale.

'They're afraid of you,' I said to Juliet, gathering up the bowl of goodies.

'You look like the devil,' she replied, taking the bowl from me.

'There's always next year,' I offered.

'I'm going to bed,' Juliet announced.

Upstairs, she tipped the fruit bowl's contents onto our bed. It made quite a spectacle. Fruity Pops. Double Lollies. Chewy Drumsticks. Fizzer Kebabs. Our open-mouth looks said it all: The children had missed out.

We wasted little time. Initially, I was quite taken by the Fizzer Kebabs' explosive tang. While Juliet couldn't seem to taste beyond the Double Lollies' gummy stubbornness. Soon we were swapping sugary descriptions, teasing one another with newly discovered flavours, nibbling from each others selections.

Then we happened upon the Love Hearts. As soon as we did everything else became a minor consideration. And we started going to bed a little earlier.

What is wrong with me? Juliet often wonders, and I jump in with my answers. I tell her she is like that Christmas child returned from Lapland, a delicate flower that has been trampled on, a girl with a crush kicked down the stairs. A comment she makes at the end of a working week lets me know I am on the right track.

'Pieces of me are breaking away,' she claims. 'At this rate there'll soon be nothing left.'

'There's no need to be like that,' I say, but she just shrugs and offers a prayer parts of me do not start breaking off too. In all likelihood this prayer will be ignored.

Secretly, however, I think Juliet invites hardship. She thrives on the fact that hers is the shopping trolley that always jams. The lily that never blooms. The flip flop that gets caught in a moving escalator. After crumpling in a heap she will drag herself back up the stairs and ask to be kicked down again. And, though she is convinced she is employed by the stupidest man in the country, this perception never prevents her setting her alarm clock.

'You need to stop chasing difficulties,' I tell her, letting my secret out of the bag.

'I can't,' she sighs. 'There are countries on my shoulders.'

'I thought you were falling apart.'

'I'm a girl,' she answers. 'I'm allowed hold two views at the same time.'

Into the bedside stereo I place a new CD - some piano sonatas by Beethoven. The timeless harmonies of the music I am sure will melt away the land masses dragging down Juliet. However, we may as well be listening to fresh air. Besides, now that she has countries on her shoulders she'd rather check out some of the 1,001 things to do before death.

'We can drive a motorbike across Mongolia,' she says. 'Take a combine harvester through the African jungles. Live in an igloo for three months.'

The igloo really appeals to her. She likes the thought of being away from everybody, ice-fishing with the Eskimos, at one with the unremitting elements. She's even starts talking about canoeing an isolated stretch of Artic Waterway.

'Edgar Allen says the death of a beautiful woman is the most poetic topic in the world,' I tell her.

'And your point is?'

'Don't look to me when you fall out of the canoe and are bitten by a king crab.'

'Oh, good! You're coming too. I'll navigate. You can paddle.'

I take this opportunity to remind her that she cannot swim. Neither of us can. Something we discovered the other night, as it happens. 'Let's go skinny-dipping,' Juliet announced on our way home. Straightaway she stripped off and galloped into the ocean. Tentatively, I followed. Ahead of me, I could see Juliet - throwing her flimsy physique upon the onrushing waves. 'Further,' she bellowed, gesturing me towards her. 'Further.'

Soon her words changed. 'I'm sinking,' she now shrieked.

When I reached her she was way out of her depth, thrashing the water as though possessed by unnatural spirits. Without warning she leaned a hand on my head and pushed me right under. 'How was the view?' she asked with a glint in her eye when we eventually scrambled back to shore. Then we popped a Love Heart. 'What does yours say?' she asked. 'Be Mine,' I answered. 'Forget it,' she replied, showing hers.

'We could bungee jump over the Angel Falls,' she says.

'More water,' I reply.

'What about trekking the deserts of Basra.'

'War zone,' I say.

'I'd love to visit the museum of deadly spiders.'

'The what?'

'It says here visitors displaying appropriate composure are allowed bunk up with the furriest spider. I suppose that would be a tarantula of some sort.'

'Juliet,' I say in my calmest voice. 'You are afraid of green flies. Two of them hopped out of our basil plant the other day and you ran upstairs. How will you cope with tarantulas?'

'Apples and oranges,' she replies.

To distract her from 1,001 things to do before death I show her a print of Van Gogh's *Irises* I picked up from our local gallery. The liberating colours I hope will unbind her from the restless whims assailing her.

'I've never seen a real iris,' she says, setting it down on the floor again. Instead she discovers fighter jets. In Lithuania they allow non-pilots fly them for thirty seconds.

'The price includes a certificate for bravery,' she remarks.

'How are you going to fly a fighter jet,' I plead. 'You can't even drive a car.'

'I was misunderstood,' she claims.

'That's always likely if you hold two views at the same time,' I tell her.

In fact neither of us can drive. We were both called to take the test on the same day – just a couple of Mondays ago. Juliet tried first. She looked right when she was turning left and a pedestrian had to duck for cover. Several minutes into my turn the tester asked me had I ever been to America. 'Why do you ask?' I answered, curious that he would question my travel habits at such a tense moment in my life. 'Because you like driving on the other side of the road,' he replied.

Juliet was devastated. 'There must be something wrong with you too,' she concluded, frowning deeply. I was so disappointed for her I enrolled us in the Last Chance Driving School. After a week of mounting kerbs, crashing gears, bickering and tears they ran us.

At the sweet shop beside the test centre we popped a couple of Love Hearts. *Too Bad* mine said. *Get a grip* said hers.

'Take an art appreciation course,' I suggest. 'Or wine tasting. Beginners Spanish perhaps. Bruising is kept to a minimum.'

'I don't have bruises.'

'If you go for a walk around Basra you will have. Not to mention permanent scarring.'

'Any scarring I have is invisible,' she says.

'I hear soul collage is very good for that.'

'We should stay right here,' she decides, pulling up the

duvet. 'Underneath the covers. Just the two of us. And never set foot outside the door again.'

So there it is. One moment she wants to traipse across the Tundra or move into an igloo. Plunge-dive a fighter jet. Hop into bed with tarantulas. Now she dare not ever again step beyond the bedroom door. Which is it to be? Then I remember what she said about the number of views girls can have at the same time.

I have her try several local remedies. Drinking. Watching golf. Walking up a mountain without shoes and socks. Upon the mountain we hunt butterflies and lapse into trances of mutual-preservation. But any relief is temporary. So we return to the bedroom.

In the bedroom, we draw the curtains, slide inside the covers, turn on our bedside lamps. For a time Juliet watches the moth dance. Switching attention to her nails she discovers there is nothing left to file. Meantime, I open my Credit Union book and discover I am broke. Again I read to Juliet. Again she reads to me. Her depictions of life before death remain completely terrifying. My rendering of Edgar Allen still lacks mystery and imagination. So we put down our books and pop a Love Heart.

'What does your say?' she asks.

'*My doll*,' I say.

'In your dreams,' she replies, sticking out her tongue.

The Girl Who Liked Words

Her name was Anne. She was a small slip of a thing with wild black hair. An acquired taste, I was led to believe, but then forever pretty. She spoke with a lilt in her voice and often paused mid-sentence in genuine wonder at the sounds issuing from her delicate throat. Sometimes she threw an arm when she spoke as though she was scattering a trail of words as she moved. And as she moved she often listed out loud what she saw or passed as though doing this brought such things into existence. She seemed to consider every word that passed her lips. She weighed these words. Some were treated like vegetables. They were diced and chopped up. Syllables were shuffled around, to produce another sound, to achieve a different effect or, as was often the case, just for the hell of it. Some were treated like naughty little children. They received a warning, were informed of their potential and then summarily clipped and put away for another day. Some words she repeated over and over, as though unsure of their worth, or trying to emphasize or establish their effects.

But some words she had only to say once. And once having had this brief outing, Anne knew they were the real deal. Words to cherish. To savour. Words that didn't wave loudly or crave centre stage or insist or wriggle across spaces occupied by less accomplished words. It was as though they were simultaneously shy and quietly aware of the effects they could achieve if someone was thoughtful enough to give them a considered utterance. And Anne had an instinct for such words for she was in possession of these same qualities herself. So she dwelt on these words and thrilled upon accidental discoveries and enjoyed her time with these special sounds.

All of this I learned from Annette, a flat mate of Anne's with whom I was staying for a couple of cram-study weeks before my repeat exams.

'You'll have to meet her,' said Annette, 'she's an interesting person. I think you'd like her. She also has exams coming up.'

I listened to some more of what Annette had to say about her flat mate. I found it all very intriguing. Though I had never considered myself a 'word' person – numbers were my poison at the time – I was attracted to parts of Anne's philosophy, especially the part about scattering words and their sounds everywhere she went, thereby acknowledging their part in the scheme of things. And though I was spoken for at the time - I had a girlfriend the other side of the country waiting for me to finish my exams - I felt that when I met Anne, that when we were introduced or when our paths collided, we could hit it off and become good friends.

For my first few days in the flat, however, we were like ships in the night. I'd get up in the morning and she'd have already left for college. I'd get in late at night and she'd have already gone to bed. If I took a lunch to college, she'd eat back at the flat. And if she stayed at college, it would be a day I remained at the flat. I wasn't unduly concerned. I was going to be here for two weeks. Getting to meet Anne, I felt, was just a matter of time. Annette agreed.

'She's a busy girl,' said Annette, 'she's hoping to do a Masters. She needs to put a portfolio together. But she'll be here tonight. You'll meet her then. She's sticking around for the weekend actually. Maybe the three of us can go for a drink. Forget about the exams for one night.'

But I had to travel to the far end of the country to visit my girlfriend. I had made promises for her birthday. I missed a good night Annette told me the following Monday morning. Her brother, John, made an appearance. He was very drunk and stared at Anne and said 'you're pretty.' He said it over and over again. Until his girlfriend arrived and took him home again.

'You've just missed Anne as well,' said Annette. 'She'll be in college all day. You should have heard her on Saturday night. It's a pity you weren't around. How was your own weekend?'

'It was okay. I didn't sleep much – although not for the reasons you're thinking, so you can take that grin off your face.'

Over breakfast Annette elaborated on Anne's penchant for words.

'She just loves words,' said Annette. 'She was here not twenty minutes ago eating breakfast and she froze with the cereal spoon on its way to her mouth and said "Peculiar, now that's an interesting word." So I asked her what's so special about it and she said, "Special, I like the texture of that word." And then out of nowhere she said, "March, doesn't that have a great sound when you really go for it – Marrrchhh. April is so soft by comparison. But a gentle encouraging word I think. It would make a great book title." She has a new word every morning, Alan, and a different thing to say about it. I think she intends to pass a comment on every word in the dictionary.'

My second week in the flat progressed in a similar fashion. I simply couldn't tally my presence in the flat with that of Anne's. It wasn't the most troubling thing to happen in my life, but I did want to meet this girl, and had already gone out of my way to discover her comings and goings. All to no avail. So I decided to stop trying to force the issue and resume my own routine. Which wasn't the worst idea in the world. My first exam date was rapidly approaching and, what with listening to all this word talk and trying to manipulate an encounter with the cause of it all, my preparation was suffering. In truth it was non-existent.

Annette became used to my unhappy knack of just missing Anne's latest appearance at the flat. She sensed my fascination with this sprite-like wisp who constantly eluded me. And Annette's own particular fascination was also becoming more apparent because whenever I now appeared, at breakfast time or very late in the evening, Annette would hail me with a one word greeting, the word she chose to greet me with being whatever word Anne was currently enthusing over. So when I appeared at breakfast time that weekend Saturday morning, with a haggard sleep-deprived look, Annette eyed me sympathetically, threw her arms in the air and said Prelude.

'And what did she have to say about it?' I asked.

'She said it was a kind word. As in possessing empathy. Oh, and that a Polish pianist had deemed it a worthy title for a piece of music he had written for a girl he loved very much.'

'I was wondering what all that humming was.'

'She was still at it heading out the door. I could hear her in the street.'

'Has she got a boyfriend?'

'Wouldn't you love to know.'

I stomped into college and for the rest of the day furthered my exam preparation in no way whatsoever.

Annette looked up from a magazine when I let myself in later that night. 'Cahoots,' she said and returned to her reading.

'You two are in cahoots is what I'm beginning to think,' I said going towards my room. 'What time is she getting up at in the morning?' I asked, determined to set my alarm one hour in advance of the answer.

'Tomorrow, I think she is due up at half past seven,' replied Annette.

'It's Sunday,' I gasped, betraying a slight tone of desperation.

'There's a book fair on in town.'

'I need to get some sleep,' I announced, and went straight to bed.

Annette was stirring porridge when I wobbled into the kitchen the following morning. I'd spent a restless night. The sun was up by the time I had finally fallen asleep and I'd yanked the cord from its socket as soon as the alarm went off. One hour later, Annette was eyeing me with a look of concern.

'I'm sorry, Alan, she was in a bit of a hurry. She ran out the door muttering book titles to herself. Oh, but she did make time for a word. Isthmus. A narrow strip or bridge, of land for example. Also there's one in your throat. She actually finds it difficult to say but, to use her own words, feels the agitated journey is worth it. She finds it both exotic and practical. And also a good name for a pet.'

I sat down and cradled my face in my hands.

'I've told her about you,' said Annette, 'and she said she is sure to be here at teatime. She wants to pour over the books she will buy today.'

'Right, that's it. I'm going to sit right here until she returns.'

I folded my arms on the table and rested my head on them. It was quiet and I must have drifted off. A warm fragrance in the air maintained my drowsy mood. I dozed for a short while and then snapped suddenly awake only for this cycle of semi-somnolence to repeat itself. A pattern soon developed. I drifted into states of intricate confusion. Instants of illumination stirred me back to consciousness. Each time a pearl of wisdom on the tip of my tongue I couldn't for the life of me retrieve.

Gradually it became more and more difficult to raise my head. It became a lead weight that seemed to loll haphazardly as though unsure of its relation to the weary body attached to it. So I eventually abandoned any efforts to steer it in any meaningful direction. It bobbled briefly and collapsed upon my still-folded arms.

At some point someone was whispering in my ear. A series of short breaths that became utterances, and finally evolved into one-syllable words. Curl. Patch. Trick. Kiss. 'Kiss who,' I said

31

and then heard the word Skiff. Afternoons spent rearranging paragraphs of numbers into equally totalling columns were starting to take their toll, I thought to myself. Then I had a nightmare. Or was I dreaming I was having a nightmare? The infinitive of the noun reconciliation was chasing me all around the college library imploring me not to ever split it. And that if I did, it would be a cold day in hell before I passed another exam. I woke up in a sweat convinced it was the morning of an exam I hadn't prepared for. My hunch was correct.

I rubbed my eyes and blinked rapidly. Annette was looking at me, giving me her most sympathetic you've-missed-her-again look.

'We tried to wake you, Alan. We nudged and shook you but you didn't stir. Anne even read aloud two chapters from a book she bought at the fair. And she actually whispered some of her favourite words in your ear.'

'Kiss,' I said, deciding that I didn't want to wake up.

'You look tired, Alan. Here, eat this. No don't get up. You're going to have to sit down for the word I'm going to tell you. It's a corker. I even think I pushed a little too hard for details myself. Are you ready? Amnion.'

'Amnion,' I repeated back to her. 'What does that mean?'

'I asked her that and she said she had no idea. She just thought of it as a word with enormous potential, one of those rare words that can soften barriers between sentences, heal rifts between paragraphs and so forth. In her own words, a word that can work miracles. She also said it wasn't necessary to know what every word means or indeed to know all the words. She said having an understanding with a few useful words is more important, and that the element of mystery in not knowing the meaning of a particular word can garner more interesting effects than a routine perusal of the dictionary. Immersing yourself in the atmosphere of a word brings you closer to its essence, she said. She told me she first heard this word amnion at a reading by a poet called Galway.'

'As in the city where I'm from Galway?'

'That's actually where this reading was. She said that this Galway fellow liked being in Galway because no one mispronounced his name. And also because he thought he was being called to a lot. Anyway, this word Amnion, she remembered it from one of his poems that night. She suggested I look it up if I really wanted to find out what it means.'

'And did you?'

'Look it up. No, I thought about it but I liked what she said about the mystery of a new word and decided that I didn't want to know. It's probably a root vegetable or something.'

'A strange looking onion I bet. Good for you but tastes horrible. I better go. I've an exam in half an hour.'

'What! You've just spent the last twenty-four hours with your head on the kitchen table. And now you've got an exam?'

'That's right – in taxation. It's not a kind sounding word, is it?'

I had no idea what to do with the numbers in the situations the examiner had set down on the buttercup yellow paper. *Buttercup yellow paper. Where did that come out of?* I read over these intriguingly put together situations several times. There were some unusual formations in the wordings. For instance, I spent maybe twenty per cent of exam time repeating to myself the term breeze block. I liked the way it wheezed along before coming to an abrupt halt. I tried saying it many times, in different ways, challenging the points of emphasis. Then a question on the topic of terminal taxation relief made me gasp audibly. The student in front of me turned around, glared in my direction and with an index finger drew a line across his throat. Isthmus, I hissed at him and he left me be again. I filled a page with numbers and bounded from the hall.

'Sanctuary,' said Annette when I walked in.

'What on earth does she see in that word?'

'She said the word sanctuary almost glows and that if you sealed it in one those space capsules and sent it away, we would find out once and for all if we share the universe with other life, because so luminous are its qualities that anything out there would be drawn to it. Tonight she said she should be home by eight.'

While I waited I took out a folder of notes for my next exam. I couldn't afford a repeat of today's fiasco. I looked at a particularly difficult problem from a past exam paper. The examiner offered the candidate two years worth of incomplete records from a four-person partnership. There was a sizeable suspense account. A full trading statement and a reconciled balance sheet were required together with detailed variance analysis in business performance between years one and two. I found myself writing out the words of this irksome problem. Suspense, reconciliation, nominal ledger, flexed budget. And then wondering what opinion Anne would have of these words. I resolved to ask her as soon as she appeared and tried to concentrate on my paper.

The numbers became a blur the more I stared at them. They started to ripple and move in mazy patterns. Then they suddenly upped off the page, paired off together and commenced bobbing frantically up and down, like black inky musical notes come to life. They performed wistful waltzes. They thrashed out a contagious siege. Like a gambolling caravan of clutter they rioted across the captious terms that had hitherto hemmed them in. Until a door slammed and they slapped themselves back onto the page again.

'Scorch,' Annette said from the far end of the room.

'What, you mean to say she's been and gone?'

'She just burst in, muttered something about a long night ahead of her, grabbed the coffee jar and bolted. And at the door, she said Scorch.'

'They're getting shorter,' was all I could say.

'I think it's exam nerves.'

By now, I was desperate for a face I could assign to all these words. I was willing to accept anyone, anything that would lead me to a form or shape responsible for my present behaviour. I said as much to my confidante.

'How many times a day do you see her,' I asked Annette. 'Can I see a photograph? Show me some of her clothes. At least let me look inside her room.'

Annette sympathized with my plight but she didn't think it a good idea for me to take my desperation into Anne's bedroom. For a few moments things became a little tense, and, thankfully, her cousin Roisín called around with her guitar. Roisín even spilled forth a memorable flurry of words, expressions and sentences and, for a time, my desperation wavered. As had my preparations for exam number two. Roisín started to teach me how to pluck a note or two on her guitar, which distracted me further. She seemed impressed by my efforts.

'Alan, there's an acoustic guitar player in you,' she said.

'Anne loves the word acoustic,' said Annette.

'That's it,' I growled. 'I've had enough. I can't take any more.'

I dropped the guitar, stormed into my room and buried my head in my accounting book.

After the exam (the less said the better) I went straight to the flat. Roisín was still playing her guitar.

'Anne's here as well,' said Roisín.

I jolted. My wobbly head instantly became a fine-tuned antenna. I gathered myself, and stepped into the kitchen where a tall fair-haired girl stood leaning against the breakfast bar, flicking through a magazine.

'Hello, I'm Anne,' she said, 'I don't think we've ever met.'

She wasn't quite what I'd been expecting. She wasn't small. She didn't have black hair. And it certainly wasn't wild. She was attractive I supposed, but not what I'd describe as pretty.

'You've changed,' I said to her.

A toilet flushed and from the bathroom, Annette's brother John appeared.

'Hiya doin' Al, I see you've met the better half. Are you right Anne, we're going to be late.'

He held the door for her, and as she passed through he turned back to me and whispered, 'I met the pretty one with the dark hair the other night. Whoooeeee, I don't know how you can get any study in with a distraction like that about the place. Gotta go. Talk soon.'

This is getting ridiculous, I said to myself. I'm never going to meet this mystery girl. That's all she is. A mystery. Like one of those words she'd rather not look up the meaning of. I wondered was the whole thing a ruse on Annette's part. But she wouldn't be so cruel at exam time. Not that it mattered much at this stage. My preparations had well and truly foundered.

I worked myself up into such a tizzy that I ransacked my room in search of a dictionary. And when I finally found one, I looked up the meaning of the word Amnion. This'll show them or her or whoever, I said aloud, tugging at pages of the flimsy page missive. I'm going to find out what this word means and shout it out from the rooftop. And then we'll see what they think of their precious mystery.

I scanned the columns of entries until I spotted the word. It was barely noticeable, actually, tucked away in between Amnesty and Amoeba. Five words elucidated its meaning, two of which I also looked up – just to be on the safe side. In the middle of all this Annette stuck her head around my door.

'What's all the commotion about?' she said.

'I'm looking up a word,' I replied in my calmest voice.

'Curiosity killed the cat,' said Annette.

'I'll be with you in a moment,' I said and motioned her from the room.

I joined her in the kitchen moments later.

'Well,' I said parking myself on a stool at the breakfast bar, 'you or your mystery friend is right.'

'About what?'

'I've just been looking up Amnion. And to be honest, I'm still not sure what exactly it is. But if Anne has discovered something in it, she can say whatever she likes about it I suppose. It's not always necessary to look the word up.'

Much later, it was still with me. I was finishing a drink in a bar, on my way to a festival reading. Three students sat at a table beside me. They were discussing a topic close to my heart.

'You want to know something else,' I heard one of them say. 'It's the only profession in the world where it is illegal to be creative.'

'Yikes,' the other two said and laughed.

I finished my drink and left for the reading. The student-talk set me thinking again about the girl I'd never met. I wondered what she was doing with her life. Had she fulfilled Annette's prophecy and passed comment on every word in the dictionary. At this stage, she'd probably moved on to other languages. French or Spanish. Maybe Farsi. It's not as if she would be concerned about translations. About the meaning of *ivresse* or *otra vez* or *la mascara es la verdadura*. Oh no. For her, these words would compel themselves into a brand new set of spells and conjurations. Forge further sounds to be in thrall to. Mysteries unnecessary to pierce.

At the reading a few words catch my attention.

'There is no sublime,' the reader says 'only the shining of the amnion's tatters.'

Applause breaks out but I can't hear a thing. To my left, two rows in front of me, I've spied the small slip of a thing with wild dark hair. She is smiling and her berry lips move delicately as she repeats what she has heard. I turn away as the poet starts to read again. And when I steal another glimpse from the seat ahead of me, the girl turns around. She looks right at me, blinks her long lash eyelids and, in a clear whimsical voice, says, 'you know I wouldn't have missed this for the whole world.'

'Neither would I,' I reply, and sit back into my seat and listen.

But it's not who I hope it will be. It never is.

Repeat Offender

Ciara tells me I have a female brain. She says: Last night when you were writing yourself reminder notes I watched a program about brains. On it they said a brain can be either male or female. They did a special test to show how. And guess what? Your brain is a girl.

I tell her I'm just a slow learner. Easily distracted. Forgetful.

'Tell me more,' she says, propping her chin in her hands, getting interested. 'Especially the bit about forgetful.'

I pay no heed to her little dig. It is a trap she is laying, and I am not going to walk into it. Not this time. Prior collisions have made me realize that, at a moment like this, there is only one course of action open to me – say nothing and keep saying it.

Latching onto the word Forgetful is very clever. She knows I am prone to the occasional dreamy lapse, and that, in spite of earnest assurances to the contrary, sooner or later, I will lapse once again. It is inevitable, Ciara says. The Repeat Offender, she sometimes calls me. It's all part of her ongoing mission to get beneath my skin. Saying I have a female brain is her latest tactic.

There are two parts to my most recent offence, possibly three. Every Friday, Ciara and I arrange to meet up after work. It's something we do to mark the start of the weekend. We might sip a coffee in Middle Street, splash out on a glass of Chardonnay along the docks or simply while away an hour browsing magazine stalls and shoe shops. Looking at shoes worries Ciara. It reminds her she does not make the best use of her feet. It also gives her an appetite. So, having worried herself through the latest styles of wedge heels, gladiator sandals and thigh-highs, she very often grabs my arm and marches me decisively to the fish shop where she treats us to a battered cod and chips. 'My feet hold the keys to the well-being of my entire body,' she might reflect between mouthfuls of chips. 'Touching them sends messages. Never touch the wrong parts,' she then cautions should I go at her with my fork. 'It will send the wrong message.'

Today, we have opted to meet for booster drinks in the new juice bar.

I committed the first part of my offence without realizing it. On this particular Friday Ciara left it to me to make the meeting-up arrangements. Thinking a teatime drink would make for a pleasant occasion, I sent Ciara to one of my two favourite pubs. Meantime, I made my way to the other, and spent a couple of lonely but satisfying drinks wondering where on earth she could be. As I propped the bar, sipping contentedly, my friend Mike appeared. He bought a round of drinks and we got to talking.

'I'm waiting for Ciara,' I said to Mike.

'Don't mention women,' Mike said. 'I was with my lover this afternoon and my wife walked in on us.'

I didn't really know what to say to this. I was hoping Mike would share more detail with me. It was obvious he was waiting for me to ask.

'What happened next?' I said.

'I started laughing,' Mike said. 'I couldn't stop. I tried to but it was no good. I buried myself beneath the bed sheets, and that made me laugh more. *What are you laughing at?* My wife asked me. Then my lover got in on the act. *Yes, Mike,* she said, *what are you laughing at?'*

'What were you laughing at?' I asked.

'I have no idea. I couldn't think of anything to say. I figured I was caught between a rock and a hard place. So I wrapped myself up further beneath the sheets. Then I noticed my *Shrek* boxer shorts. They were tangled up beneath the sheets too. Shrek was grinning away, giving me a look that said *I told you so.* That made me laugh more. I laughed so much I made myself thirsty. And here I am.'

During this revealing anecdote a text message came through to my phone. *Where are you?* It was from Ciara. *Waiting for you* I texted back.

'What are you going to do?' I asked Mike, thinking he wasn't quite ready to finish his piece of news.

'I am going to have four pints of Guinness and three large glasses of red wine. Then I will clear my head,' Mike said. 'I'm thinking Sardinia.'

'Sardinia?' I repeated after him.

'Sardinia,' he replied. 'I will go to Sardinia and clear my

head. It should take about a month.'

I was about to ask one last question, but just at that moment our mutual friend Eugene showed up. His face was red and sweating, and he looked thirsty too. At once, he put a round of drinks on the counter, raised his hands and cleared his throat as though in preparation for an inspirational speech.

'A woman has moved into the flat above me,' he growled.

'Don't mention women,' Mike said, and Eugene raised his glass to acknowledge a vital piece of advice.

'I have to mention this woman,' he then said, continuing to growl.

'Go ahead so,' Mike conceded. 'But get straight to the point.'

'This woman,' Eugene continued, shaking his sweaty head. 'She is frightening. Every night she opens her bedroom window, pushes herself right out into the darkness and calls out the word Naked. She isn't wearing any clothes when she does it. She has a very seductive voice.'

During this bizarre anecdote the call came through.

'Where are you?' Ciara wanted to know.

'Still waiting for you,' I let her know back, and she hung up.

After that things became a little vague. I listened to some more about Eugene's seductive neighbour. More familiar faces arrived into the pub, rounds of drinks steadily accumulated, and I enjoyed further episodes of doomed romance and perplexing behaviour. At the time I remember thinking about all the juicy stories I would have for Ciara when she finally showed up.

I like meeting up with Ciara. I work as an assistant obituaries editor, most of my work I do from home, and, come half past four on Friday, am only too happy to abandon whatever obituary it is I am involved with and make the three mile trek into town. I like walking as it helps to rid my mind of the sombre words I key into my laptop. The final mile I particularly enjoy, as it is all downhill and there are no cemeteries.

Ciara, herself, works quite close to town, in an accounts office. Her employer is a wealthy man. He owns fourteen businesses and has a manager for each of them. Ciara works under the manager of the timber business. He says things like *How would you like to become part of a team to revolutionize timber? We need to move from the divergent to the convergent. Send me some key words and action plans.* He also likes to drop into conversation that he is seeing someone with interests in Silicon Valley. Ciara spends a lot of her time seeking out key words for the timber revolution. She sends on various candidates to her manager, together with action plans. *That action is resolution evasive* she often hears back. By the time Friday evening arrives Ciara can be in a crazy mood. Sending her to the wrong pub is not wise.

In the new juice bar I skim down through the menu card. While Ciara looks about her, taking in the bar's adventurous layout.

'This is quirky,' Ciara says when the juice lady arrives to take our orders. The juice lady beams as she reaches behind her ear for a pen.

'I'll have a *Pink Passion*,' I say.

'Me too,' Ciara says happily, obviously pleased with today's choice of meeting place.

'How goes the timber revolution?' I venture once Ciara has finished admiring the surroundings and the juice lady has left again.

'Oh, great,' she replies. 'This afternoon there was a lot of sighing over one of my action plans. It was put to me I need to experience a light-bulb moment.'

'A girl from the bank said as much to me earlier,' I say. '*Put spring into your cash* she said the second I picked up the phone. Then she offered me lots of money for the lowest ever fee. All I have to do is decide that I need a hydrogen-concept car, a home in Transylvania or a two-year long around-the-world cruise. Two years is the new one year, the girl told me. She had a very seductive voice. I was tempted.'

'Maybe it's the girl now living above Eugene,' Ciara comments, and straightaway, I kick myself for making reference to my recent night on the town.

'Two ladies from the Legion of Mary came knocking too,' I continue, as the juice lady sets down our *Pink Passions*. 'They knocked and knocked and demanded to know why I had left the church. *We will say a decade together*, they said, and lobbed a stack of beads at me. Ladies, I pleaded, putting a hint of panic in my voice. I have a girl waiting for me on the kitchen table. She is armed, voluptuous and unpredictable. Right now, I don't have time for a decade.'

'Did they believe you?' Ciara asks.

'They doused me with holy water and made a bee-line for the neighbour. Don't knock on that door, I called after them, he thinks hell is other people.'

'You stole my line,' Ciara says, reaching for her drink.

'I could do worse. For all you know there might have been a girl on the kitchen table.'

'Sometimes I think you're not all that with it,' Ciara says, slurping into her drink.

I wasn't all that with it when I started into the second part of my recent offence. Eventually that night, after many drinks, my friend Mike and I went our separate ways. But not before his lover made a surprise appearance in the pub and bought a final round of drinks. 'I love this woman,' Mike said as she placed a pint of Guinness in front of him. Extra surprising was the near-simultaneous arrival of Mike's wife who picked up the pint and threw it into Mike's face. 'Don't mention women,' I said to her, wobbling uncertainly from the bar. After that I let the night air take me.

Having staggered my way home, I tried to water down my inconsideration, and, though I was incoherently charming, I did have a remote feeling that taking this approach would not be acceptable. The little devil standing behind me prodded me on regardless, and I put down my lapse entirely to a minor communication glitch. 'Mobiles,' I tut-tutted with emphasis, fumbling my way through rogue money notes and loose change, in order to unearth the cause of our aborted evening together. 'The ruination of intimacy,' I said, holding aloft the trouble-making gadget and scolding it with the index finger of my other hand. To quarry my way out of what was fast becoming a hopeless situation I even ventured an attempt at humour. This is when the second part of my offence really kicked in. 'It's your fault for letting me make the arrangements,' I said to Ciara. I've been hearing all about it since.

'Several brochures arrived this afternoon,' I say, taking a mouthful of my juice. 'All sorts of things. They flew right in through the letterbox. All except one addressed personally to you. But I opened them anyway.'

'Opening somebody else's mail is a sin,' Ciara says.

'That's not right,' I answer. 'Polluting the environment is a sin. Genetic modification. Putting a divide between rich and poor. And becoming obscenely wealthy. Stuff like that. But not opening somebody else's mail. That's just breaking the law.'

'You and your sins,' Ciara sighs. 'You sound just like my mother.'

'You have received a privilege card from Time Magazine,' I tell her. 'It offers you a 54-issue subscription at a guaranteed low rate. They're throwing in a complimentary deluxe encyclopaedia Britannica. A fleece. And six additional months of Time – think what you could do with that. The brochure not addressed to you was flogging an online interactive brain training program. It assures me that if I play my cards right I can become a Thought Leader. At long last I will be able to progress my mind. There. What do you think of that?'

'Make sure you tell them it's a female mind,' Ciara says.

'That doesn't matter. Adhering to their twelve week program will assist me do what I always say I'm going to do. The world will come alive for me without recourse to five glasses of wine. In time to come I will no longer not know precisely what it is I am apologizing for.'

'Oh,' she says. 'I don't envy your chances with that last one.'

Not being able to articulate how my blatant no-show and later attitude could upset Ciara so much evolved, over the course of that particular weekend, into the third, and hopefully, final part of my recent offence. This was deemed my worst violation. Indeed, I have been since told that were it not for my mammoth ability to deny any wrongdoing, the entire episode would, at this stage, be long since forgotten about. So, in a way, I suppose my wrongdoing is still evolving.

Initially, I didn't offer an apology because I was busy trying to worm my way out of the situation. Plus, I wasn't yet convinced an apology was what she was looking for. 'We swapped text messages,' I argued. 'We weren't far away from each other,' I stressed. 'You should have known where to find me,' I threw in as a last ditch token of resistance. As I proceeded to dig myself into a deeper pit, any notions of repentance slipped quietly into the more desolate regions of my mind. At one point, I was asked to prove that I was a man. 'Show me your balls,' Ciara screamed at me from a place lazily described as being not for the faint-hearted. 'Go on, show me.' It was then that I noticed Ciara had acquired prosecuting eyes and was digging her longest fingernails deep into the palms of her hands. It seemed to me that the best thing I could do was to try to get away in one piece. So I offered up the necessary gesture.

'Tell me what it is you're sorry for,' she demanded, but I didn't have the energy to back it up with explanatory detail. I just stood there, hopping from one foot to another, my parched tongue hanging out of my mouth like a thirsty dog itching to get away from its over-fussy master. So my apology was thrown out. Queries about advance apologies for future occasions were thrown out too.

'Whenever there is a gaping hole in the road in front of us, you do not walk around it. You jump straight in.' This is what she said to conclude our showdown. I thought it wise to let her have the last word.

'A lady called and read me the riot act for covering her pizza with jalapeno peppers,' I say, splashing through the remains of my juice. 'I don't know anything about jalapeno peppers, I tried telling her, I'm an obituarist. *I'd look for a different career if I were you*, she said back to me. Then, and you're not going to believe this, a young lad walked right in through the front door. He was carrying a pizza. He marched through the hallway, sat down at the kitchen table and started eating the pizza.'

'Our house must resemble a pizza shop,' Ciara says, rolling her eyes.

'Another guy managed to sell me a Christmas tree.'

'It's the middle of September,' Ciara says, now spreading her arms.

'He said he would throw in a sprig of holly,' I say.

'That seals it,' Ciara concludes. 'Your brain is female all the way through.'

Though she has an unhappy knack of always seeing holes in the road, I enjoy sharing with Ciara these little moments from my day. Over time, this over-and-back between us has become a habit. A minor ritual we enact that, on the one hand, provides me with an opportunity to engage with a living person and, on the other, removes Ciara from the prescriptive routines of her own working life. And though she often wearies of my sluggish mind, in her own way I'm sure Ciara looks forward to hearing what I will have to say. The empathetic look on her face later that evening says as much, as I make awkward attempts to massage her neglected feet.

My favourite was the call I got from a murderer. No sooner

had I picked up the receiver than she was shouting hysterically down the line. *I have a man beside me,* she screamed. *He's sitting in a pool of his own blood. I didn't mean to do it.* Then the voice changed from hysterical screaming to urgent justification. *He pushed me. He pushed and pushed until finally I cracked. I went over the edge.* By now, she was sobbing heavily over the phone line, and throughout my attempts to find out more details she continually repeated her justification. *He had it coming,* she said. *He ignored all my warnings.* She said the bit about ignoring her warnings in such a way that made it seem ignoring warnings was just about the worst thing her victim could have done. Before I could get in another word she hung up. I was a little shaky after the call, and took a few moments before putting through a call to the emergency number. I explained the situation as best I could. They thanked me for being so conscientious.

'Don't be such a drama queen,' Ciara said, when I told her all about it. But later that night they called me back. The emergency hotline, that is. Ciara was there to witness it. It turns out we have a phone number that is the same number as the emergency hotline in a coastal town fifty miles away. The only difference is the final digit of the prefix. The coastal town has a four; ours is a one. 'That's it,' Ciara concluded, 'we need to arrange a new phone number.' But I didn't want to. 'Think of all the interesting phone calls we'll miss out on,' I said, gesticulating wildly. 'You are damaged goods,' Ciara said. 'What I see is not what I get. There are hidden things inside you.' 'What things?' I asked. 'How should I know?' she replied. 'They're hiding.'

It was Ciara who suggested I start writing myself reminder notes. She even volunteered to write some of them for me. So come Thursday night, as I set about locating the special points of her feet, she writes a reminder that will help me not mess up the following day. *Stop giving Ciara misleading information.* While she's at it she pens further notes, notes that will assist my immersion into days to come. She pens these notes in such a way that will make me sit up and take heed. *Stop making bets you cannot win. Stop answering the door to daytime sellers. Stop letting them sell you things you do not need. Stop beginning your day with imaginary conversations.* You could say the notes are designed so as to avoid trouble a little further down the line, not unlike preventative medical tests. In my case they are to ensure I don't lapse yet again. The way things are going I cannot risk another lapse.

My friend Mike can't stop laughing when I tell him all about it a couple of Fridays later. I still don't know what it is he finds so funny all the time, and asking him for an explanation is pointless. Laughing isn't taken seriously enough, is all he has to say.

'That may be but I'm running low on get-out-of-jail-free cards,' I tell him.

'Don't mention women,' he says, putting a pair of pints and two large glasses of red wine on the counter. At once I get the feeling he has a lengthy story he would like to share, and, without really thinking about it, I switch off my mobile phone.

'I've been given an ultimatum,' he begins, scarcely able to keep a straight face.

Liar, Liar

Yoou'll make a great criminal,' my father says to me. I laugh when he says it. 'I'm serious. You have an honest face,' he goes on. I don't think what he says is funny but I don't know how else to react. I don't even know why he says it. Is it because he's always in trouble himself? He gets away with nothing. Especially when he tells Mum different places he has to be. She never says anything but she doesn't have to. Lines appear on her forehead and I know he's in trouble. The lines always spell trouble.

'I have to go playing squash and I'm late,' he said last week before he went rushing out the door. But when he was gone, Mum found his racket in the cloakroom and the lines appeared.

'Mary asked me to look at her cistern but I won't be long,' he said the other evening. But when Mum met Mary at the vegetable shop and asked her about the cistern, Mary looked very confused. 'I haven't got a cistern,' Mary said and a few lines appeared on her forehead too. Then the two of them stood there spelling trouble with their lines. Right in front of the vegetable man, who was smiling away waiting for them to buy cabbage and onions.

'I have to give a night class to the Leaving Certs,' he says tonight, heading out the door. But Mum just rolls her eyes up towards her forehead, as though all that concerns her are the trouble-making lines.

As far as I'm concerned it doesn't matter whether he's playing squash without a racket or teaching Leaving Certs in the middle of the night or looking at cisterns that aren't there. When he comes home he's always happy. It doesn't even matter what time it is. He sails in through the door with his brown paper bag and happy face like someone with a new toy. And the later it is the happier he is. He's like a brand new man. I know all this because I'm always up – waiting for the gate to rattle and the key to scratch at the front door. It's a great time to get him talking. He doesn't do a lot of it during the day. He's a bit like me like that. 'Talk,' he says to me at dinner time and I laugh because I never know what to say when he asks me to. I never feel like talking. Except late at night, when everybody else is in bed, and he comes home with his paper bag and happy breath. I can never wait to hear what he has to say about who he met or where he was or what he plans to do next.

'Let's go into the kitchen,' he always says, cracking open the bottle he has brought home and putting his finger to his lips to keep down the noise. 'We're partners in crime,' he says, taking a slurp of his drink. I'm always hoping he'll bring me home a bottle of Fanta. That way we can both slurp and we'll be proper partners in crime.

When he is out I stay up and watch the old black and white films. Everyone else is in bed and I like watching them on my own. That way no-one interrupts with stupid questions about what is happening or why is that fellow getting riddled or can they switch the channel when they get fed up. I never get fed up. I love watching them. Gangster films with James Cagney and Edward G. Robinson. I love saying that name. Edward G. Robinson. I think I'm great when I say it because nobody else knows who he is. Nobody except my partner in crime. He used to watch the films with me before he started going out. It was him who first got me interested in them. And he knows everything about them. All the actors and who made the film and when it was made. 'That film is older than me,' he says. He remembers all the lines and can do impressions. He must have seen them all at this stage.

'So. Tell me what you watched tonight,' he asks me, when he comes home.

'*The Public Enemy*,' I say and he starts.

'That's a marvellous film,' he says. 'I'd say it's older than me and you and everyone else put together. It's nearly as good as *Angels With Dirty Faces*.'

'That's on next week,' I tell him.

'Isn't James Cagney terrific,' he says. Then he does his impression. He puts down his bottle, scrunches up his face and makes a gun with his fingers. 'You dirty rat,' he says, pointing his gun at me. 'You dirty stinking little rat.' Then he fires his gun. Rat-tat-tat-tat-tat. And I can't stop giggling.

In my room I scrunch up my face like Edward G. Robinson. I snarl at my blue piggybank as I get ready to talk. Except I use

James Cagney's lines. Besides, Edward G. Robinson is older than James Cagney, so I should be the younger man.

'Shut up oinking or you won't breathe anything. Not even air,' I say to my piggybank. 'Do you hear me pig?' I say and let piggy have it. Rat-tat-tat-tat-tat. Then I pull out the plastic plug and let my coin collection spill out onto the floor.

When I see James Cagney drink glasses of milk in *Angels With Dirty Faces*, I run into the kitchen and fill a glass. In no time, I love milk. I drink glasses and glasses of it. And I chomp bananas. James Cagney eats bananas as well. But the police kill him at the end of the film, even though the Dead End Kids love him, and I'm not too happy about that.

'Those dirty stinking cops,' says my partner in crime when he comes home.

He's in a great mood for talking tonight. I never know what to expect and that's part of the fun.

'I tell you what,' he says, 'we'll move to America. What do you think of that idea?'

America. Home of all the best gangsters. Edward G. Robinson and James Cagney. Peter Lorre who sounds like a snake. Sydney Greenstreet who's as big as a balloon. And George Raft who even looks like a gangster. Well if he thinks I'll make a good criminal there's no better place to be to learn the ropes. Because that's what I have to do if I want to be a criminal. Learn the ropes. I hope we move before the mood goes off him.

The following morning I'm sitting at the table, waiting for him to break the news to everyone about moving to America. But he just stares at the cup of tea on the table in front of him, as though reaching out for it is a step beyond him. I know it's our secret, so I say nothing either. Then he goes upstairs to get ready for work.

'At what time did you go to bed?' Mum asks me, and I say I was in bed early.

'Did you hear your father come home?' she asks, and I say I was asleep.

'Stop making things up,' she says and I go upstairs.

'I'm not a rat,' I say to my mirror. 'Partners in crime don't rat on each other.'

He still hasn't said anything about America because it's not time to go. I know why it isn't time. He has to save money before we can go. That's what I'm told any time I want to go somewhere. You have to save money. Which is what I'm trying to do. And I know he doesn't like being asked questions, like where he was last night and what time he came home. So I leave it at that.

Before I leave the house I stash piggy under my bed. 'As much as squeak and I'll drill you full of lead,' I say. Then I turn to my mirror. 'I'm going to make a great criminal,' I say. 'From now on, no more Mr. Nice Guy.'

At school I let Sr. Beatrice know I'm armed and dangerous. Down town, I run into the bank and say 'stick em up.' On my way home, I splash in mucky puddles and smear dirt all over my honest face. 'I'm the Dead End Kid,' I say when people look at me. 'Now SCRAM!'

Everybody believes me, no matter what I say. They're all quaking in their boots. The only person who doesn't is Mum. He isn't able to fool her either. So I don't feel so bad about that. 'Why is my purse empty?' she asks and he has to shout before she listens to him.

Upstairs in my room I feel sorry for him and laugh at the same time. I spin my globe and pick a place in the world where I'd like to be. I like being in other places. Especially when I hear him shouting. When that happens, I don't really want to be a criminal – I just want to be some place else. Like America. But it looks like I'll have to be a gangster in America because it's the only thing I'm good at. Anyway, I like him saying I'll be a great criminal. It makes me feel important.

'Are you going out tonight?' I ask him later, hoping he'll say yes. Because then I can look forward to when he comes home. It's like one person goes out the door and another comes back. And I always know which one I prefer.

'What's on tonight?' he asks me, before he heads out.

'Something called *Casablanca*,' I say.

'Bogart is in that,' he replies, making a funny shape with his lips. 'Here's looking at you kid,' he says. Then he winks at me and disappears out the door.

The film starts. Mum hears the TV and tries to get me to bed. Then she sees the film and sits up and watches it too.

It's not really a gangster film. There are some boring parts in it like when Bogart gets interested in the girl who keeps asking Sam to play the song. But then Bogart wants to hear the song too. I don't know why they keep asking for the song because it only makes them sad. 'Couldn't you cry,' Mum says and I wish she would clear off. It's the girl's fault for starting it and I wish she would clear off too. But she isn't going anywhere. At least not until the end. Everybody likes Bogart. Even his enemies. *I stick my neck out for nobody*, he says but I think he's telling lies.

He's always telling lies and getting away with it. He even fools Mum and she never believes anything. So, apart from the bit with the girl, I really want to be like Bogart.

'Humphrey Bogart was born on Christmas Day 1899,' Mum tells me when it's over. 'Imagine that.' Then she reaches for a hanky.

'Why does everyone like him?' I ask.

'They like him because he's honest,' she says.

'But he's a liar. How can he be honest if he's telling lies?'

Then I hear the key in the door. We both do.

'Time for bed,' Mum says through her hanky.

'Where's my partner in crime going?' he says when he sees me heading up the stairs. 'Do you know what we'll do tomorrow? We'll go to Galway. We'll all get up early and go to Galway.'

But he stays in bed and Mum brings me to the shops. I hate going to the shops and ask Mum what about going to Galway. She makes out like it's the craziest idea she ever heard. Instead she makes me try on a sleeveless jumper in the clothes shop. I twist my face into a scowl. Snarl at blousy women who look my way. Spit fierce words at the checkout girl who dares cross my path. All the time I wish I was in Galway. Or America. Getting up to no good with my partner in crime. Then I think of something else.

'I need apples and bananas,' Mum says to the vegetable man. The vegetable man fills his scales and keeps a sharp eye on me. So I don't try anything.

'Ninety-five Euros please, mam,' he says when he hands over the apples and bananas.

'Ninety-five Euros? You dirty rat,' I say. I say it under my breath because the vegetable man doesn't look like someone I should mess with. That's who the vegetable man reminds me of. Especially with the cigarette hanging out of his mouth. Anyway, Mum is on to him. She doesn't even give him one Euro for the apples and bananas.

'My mistake, your fault,' he says to Mum taking the money.

'Liar, liar,' she says back and they both laugh.

'The vegetable man is a gangster,' I tell her on the way to Dunnes Stores.

In Dunnes, I have a better chance. There is a queue to pay and we have a basket full of shopping. All the chocolate bars and chewing-gum are kept beside the till. While Mum is unloading her basket, I slip a packet of Juicy Fruit in my pocket. No one sees a thing. James Cagney would be proud of me. The Public Enemy. At large in Dunnes Stores.

As soon as we get home I fill a glass of milk. I reach into my pocket and feel the packet of chewing-gum. I head for my room to stash it. As I walk in I can hear my pig of coins jingling around.

'I need it for the rent-man,' he says. 'I'll give it back to you next week.'

I don't say anything because I've taken Juicy Fruit from Dunnes Stores. We're both in it up to our necks. 'It's all part of being a criminal,' I tell piggy, when I'm alone again.

'You've got to watch *The Roaring Twenties*,' he tells me later. Then he tells Mum he has to go to see the doctor about his bad back for a few minutes.

He's right. *The Roaring Twenties* is really fast moving. I'm really enjoying the police chasing the hoodlums across the city. And the Tommy guns shooting fire. It doesn't look like James Cagney will make it. Everybody is out to double-cross him. Even his friends don't trust him. Then a car screeches. It's outside our house. Then my partner in crime is inside. He's out of breath and trying to say something. His speech is slurry. So it takes him a few goes.

'Two men are going to knock on this door,' he says. 'Tell them I've been here all night. Ok.'

Then the bell rings. I open the door and two Guards stand on the front step. I'm praying that they don't know about the Juicy Fruit. What if someone in Dunnes Stores has noticed a missing packet of chewing gum? Then we'll both be in a tight spot.

'Goodnight young fellow. Is your father in?'

'Of course he is. He's been here all night.'

'Are you sure about that?' the other one asks.

'Is it not past your bedtime?' says the first one.

'My dad let me stay up to watch *The Roaring Twenties*,' I say. 'We both watched it. I'm the Dead End Kid.'

They look at each other and then at me. Then they look over my shoulder.

'I'd say there's a pair of you in it,' says the first Guard and I see him wink at the other one. 'Eh, sonny. As thick as thieves.'

They shrug at each other and walk off. This time they're not going to get James Cagney.

In the kitchen he's falling around the place. Slapping me on the back. Slapping his own knee. Saying I knew it and I told you so and cracking open a bottle and letting it spill all over the kitchen floor. He's in the best mood I ever saw.

'Not a word to your mother,' he says, crossing his lips and tapping his nose.

I copy him to let him know my lips are sealed. Then I show him the Juicy Fruit and tell him all about it. He can't believe it. And he's off again. Telling me stories about what he used to get up to when he was a boy. Stealing silver spoons from hotels and eating meals in restaurants without paying for them and pretending he was going to do loads of things that he never did. And he looks down at the floor. At the small puddle he's let spill out of his bottle in all the excitement. And he shakes his head slowly as though he's sorry he spilt it. And it's quiet in the kitchen. Just like it is during the day.

So here we are. Sitting up at the counter. Nodding our secrets at each other. Him cracking open a bottle and me with my glass of milk. As thick as thieves. James Cagney and the Dead End Kid. Partners in crime.

Billabong

y mother has just returned from a month in Australia. She made the twenty-four hour plane journey to see my sister, who has emigrated. She stayed in Australia for one full month. She says the entire experience was a privilege. She also keeps saying the word Billabong. There is a slight inflection in her voice when she says it.

'It's an aboriginal word for water hole,' she tells me.

'So it's a pub,' I say.

'Don't be facetious,' she clips. 'Throughout the arid landscapes of Australia it represents a source of survival.'

'Just like pubs,' I say to her.

'Nothing could be further from the truth,' she exclaims. 'Everything is different.'

She sounds like my sister and I become suspicious.

My sister lives in Sydney, in a neighbourhood called Newtown, outside of which I hear she never steps. I can't understand this. All that way to settle in a place she never strays from. But my mother is adamant. 'It's so different,' she says. 'I could have spent another month there.'

I look up Newtown in my concise atlas. I plunder an old Geography of Ireland. I can locate a Newtown in nearly every county in the country.

'What's so different about it?' I ask but I think she misunderstands the question.

Instead, she is awash with information about Sydney. And there is a gradual escalation in her inflecting as she shares with me the key details of her trip.

'Along either shoreline of the famous harbour there are countless walking trails and coves and hideaways that have been carved out over time from the coastal rocks,' she tells me. 'A wild tangled weed called lantana thrives along these coastal trails. Isn't that a lovely word?'

And there's more.

'Beside the famous opera house, the Domain Gardens are full of giant fig trees from which dangle clusters of fruit bats until twilight. Then they launch themselves out over the harbour waters and form sinister silhouettes against the fading light.'

And there's more.

'Groups of individuals climb the arch of the famous harbour bridge. They stand at the highest point and look like tiny dots. They must have a fantastic view from there.'

And there's more.

She has tasted barramundi. She has heard the parakeet. She has seen swathes of purple wisteria.

'I also saw a frill-necked lizard,' she says. 'It looked like a miniature dinosaur.'

'Where did you see that?' I ask.

'In the Chinese Gardens,' she says.

'In Australia?' I say back to her but she ignores me. 'There's a movie called Lantana,' I continue, trying to put a clamp on this endless list. 'It's set in and around Sydney.'

'I'll have to see it,' she says.

'Some of the characters seem to be in a right tangle,' I tell her.

'Billabong,' she says and, thankfully, disappears to do some unpacking.

Of course, I'm sure I know why she has latched onto this particular word. It is a reminder to her of her exotic trip, something she may never again get the chance to do. Time passes, loose chipping accumulates, as she claims herself. But as well as this, my mother likes words. And new words are a special treat. She's always on the lookout for one. Years ago, my sister and I discovered her half way up a great oak tree. 'A famous poet carved a message into this tree,' she called down to us through the branches. My sister and I looked at each other and giggled. Another time, just outside Sligo, a long haulage truck pulled out of a circus field right in front of us. 'Look what it says on the back of that lorry,' she said, slamming on the brakes of our car, but just then an elephant crossed in front of us and blocked my view. She is constantly drawn to obscurely positioned slogans, is always reading unnecessary notices and, in her eternal quest for a new word, also listens to other people's conversations. She seems to derive a genuine kick from the word selections she witnesses. *Twenty three and a half hour daily delivery service*, she later told me was what she read off the transport lorry.

After some more lists, as I knew she would, she gets around to the weather. And how different the climate is in Australia. How warm it is – all the time. How blue the endless skies are – all the time. But it's the weather forecast she seems most interested in talking about. 'In Australia,' she begins, 'if all the gorgeous sunshine is going to be briefly interrupted, the weatherman will say *today it will rain for a few minutes*. Over here, if all the rain is going to be briefly interrupted, the weather lady says *today it will be dry for a lot of the time*. I think that's really funny.'

I knew straightaway the weather lady my mother had in mind. She is the Mother of Doom. As soon as she appears after the news you just know we've had it. Irrespective of her silver linings and rose tinted glasses. So, in a way, I had to agree with my mother. Not that I let her know. My suspicions as to her wellbeing were proving to be correct. I had never before heard her sound with such attitude and purpose. The inflecting was continuing. And the word Billabong seemed destined to make an appearance in every conversation. It was a good job she hadn't stayed away any longer, I said to myself. If she had, I quietly reasoned, she might have returned speaking a completely incomprehensible language. And her voice might have entirely changed. And that definitely didn't bear thinking about.

As well as latching on to new words and enthusing over unusual phrasings from everyday life, my mother occasionally spices her linguistic pot by throwing in a dash from Shakespeare or adding a pinch from a favourite poem. It's not something done to impress. Nor is it calculated. A rich aphoristic medley is liable to issue forth at any time as though the most obvious at-the-time utterance. Amidst the latest bursts of this aboriginal word she is currently peddling, she has just said, 'unless you become aware of your stupidity, you'll never learn how to use your knowledge.'

'What's that from?' I ask her but she shrugs her shoulders.

'It was a line written on a blackboard outside a bookshop in Newtown. You should have seen the bookshops. I didn't realise there were so many Australian writers. This line was on the blackboard for four days. I noticed that they used to change the line daily. But they left that one be for some reason.'

'Maybe it was for the tourists,' I say and quickly add, 'how is my darling sister?'

'Oh she looks great. She really enjoys life in Sydney. She loves Newtown. It's full of energy. I think she'll stay there. She brought me to every place I wanted to see. The Opera House. Bondi Beach. The weekend markets. But what's been going on here?' she asks me as though she has become suddenly aware of a certain absentmindedness.

'You haven't missed a thing,' I tell her. 'It's dry for a lot of the time. Down the road there is three quarters of a wall for sale – it will set you back twenty thousand. Oh, and someone keeps ringing up from a water purification company offering you 35 Euros towards beauty if you let him come and show you all the impurities in your tap water. He seems very keen.'

And she's off again.

'There is a river in Australia where you can dip in your cup and drink to your heart's content,' she says. 'And near this river slithers the fearsome snake – the most dangerous snake in the world.'

'Thank God for Saint Patrick,' I reply.

'Australia's got it all,' says my mother. 'In shops they have unwanted film canisters you can use to tip your cigarette ash.'

'Smoking is banned,' I tell her.

'In ice-cream parlours you can get a cup of coffee poured over a scoop of ice-cream.'

'As if it isn't brutal enough on its own,' I say.

'You can get the most delicious Greek salad.'

'In Australia?' I say back to her.

'The people are so pleasant,' she continues, ignoring me, 'there is so much to do. And the weather is just glorious – all the time. It gets really hot. I was constantly thirsty. I never drank so much water. I brought loads of it everywhere we went. Your sister said I could open a water shop and call it Jean's Water.'

'Billabong,' I say to her without thinking and she laughs.

But I'm becoming quite concerned now. She is just too invigorated. It cannot be good for her. Before she always spoke in a gentle easy-listening fashion. She never attempted to put her words to music - she knows she can't carry a note to save her life. But at this stage even her most humdrum assertions seem to require soprano delivery. And this Billabonging is putting the fetters on me. She keeps saying it. Every so often. Out of the blue. With no obvious connection to anything being said at the time.

I tell her I'm starting a Billabong box. Like a swear box, except it's for the word Billabong as opposed to a swear word. I set the ante at a fiver. Pretty soon it's up to 25. Then 50. Then 75.

Then she shows me a couple of tops she has brought back as gifts. Damn it if the brand name isn't Billabong.

'They're exploiting the aborigines,' I point out.

'Don't be facetious,' she says and snatches them from me.

But they look great. They have vibrant colours in interesting combinations.

'Clothing that guarantees good health,' my mother asserts, presenting them to me again, when she sees I'm impressed.

Examining my gifts, I notice she has forgotten to remove the price tags.

'Good health is costly,' I tell her.

'Billabong,' she replies.

After a week or so she will be back to normal, I keep reassuring myself. Which is just as well as I will soon have to leave myself. And, in spite of her current elation, she does look a little tired around the eyes, something I hadn't noticed before her trip. Then again, she has had to contend with my sister for the past four weeks.

But I can't help thinking that the experience has gone to her head a little. Maybe it's nothing more than a severe form of jet lag that needs to run its course – I hope so. Maybe that fierce snake or frilly lizard managed to get a hold of her – I hope not. Maybe I need to become more aware of my stupidity in order to get to the heart of the matter. Or, dare I say it, could it be that there is something in the water *down under*. By all accounts she drank an awful lot of it. In any event her current state of mind leaves me with much to ponder.

A couple of days later, as I continue to mull over the prevailing conditions of my existence, she sits down beside me and announces that next week she is going to Denmark.

'What,' I reply, sure that I haven't correctly heard her. Nevertheless, I repeat word for word what she has just said to me. 'Did you just say that next week you are going to Denmark?'

'I always wanted to see the Little Mermaid,' she says.

'I need a drink,' I reply in desperation.

'Billabong,' she says, with an aura of someone who has lived a long time, inflecting a little further.

The Lake-Isle

For a long time it has been just Mother and me. So long I can't remember what it was like before. If anyone ever came to visit. If the telephone ever rang. If I had a brother or a sister. A father. When I ask Mother she throws up her arms and goes into the kitchen. She throws open the doors of the baking cupboard, grabs her mixing bowl and turns on the stereo really loud. She does a lot of throwing and I know it's time to stop asking questions.

We live together in a house just around the corner from the Riverside. It's a two storey house with two rooms downstairs – the kitchen and the sitting room - and two rooms upstairs – our bedrooms. Peter Corless lives in the house beside us - with a Labrador called Arthur Guinness. Other people live further up the road. But I only know Peter and his dog.

Sometimes Mother wants me out of the house. 'Stay away from me,' she says. 'I'm in my sin.' When she's in her sin I go up the Riverside and try to remember what it was like before. The

Riverside is my favourite place. It's calm and peaceful. I watch the row boats bobbing on the water. The ducks yakking about God knows what. The midges colliding. Now and then I get frustrated and pelt the swans with stones. They stand up in the shallows and shake their white feathers at me. But I'm not afraid, and get ready to box them with my clenched fists. Then they spread their wings and fly. I watch them fly. I like the way they move through the air. They look graceful and I'm sorry I threw stones. Then I strip off, wade into the water and swim like a fish. I don't remember learning how to swim but I do it very well. The water is freezing but I don't notice the cold. I never do. There is water as far as the eye can see.

The Riverside is a good place to meet people. I like it that it's just Mother and me at home. But when she's in her sin I like to see who else there is to talk to. 'Here comes Mastermind,' they say when I appear along the Riverside. Mastermind. That's what they call me. On account of all my knowledge.

'What is the capital of Nicaragua?' Peter Corless asks me when we pass each other.

'Managua,' I say.

'Do you hear that Arthur Guinness?' he says, shaking his head at his Labrador. 'Managua.'

'How long is the River Nile?' asks Fintan Power from the Water View Hotel.

'Four thousand one hundred and eighty four miles,' I say.

'Four thousand one hundred and eighty four miles,' he repeats after me like he is a parrot.

'I have a question,' begins Nessa Flynn from Harmony Hill. 'Do you know where you are going? There's no need to answer.

I'm sure you know exactly where you are going. But let me tell you anyway. All the way to the top. That's right. You are going all the way to the top.'

'The top of what,' I wonder, and she smiles and wags her waxy finger at me.

'How many of them honours things did you get in the Junior Cert?' she then asks and I have to tell her I'm not doing it 'til next year.

'Well you should do it this year,' she says, still wagging the finger. 'You have more brains than the entire road and don't let anyone tell you otherwise.'

'Yes Mrs. Flynn,' I say with a chuckle because I know she is about to start into people without brains.

'Look at that eejit Fintan Power. His rich daddy built him a hotel and now he thinks his name is Hilton. He wouldn't know how to manage two horses at a donkey derby. If brains were made of chocolate that fellow wouldn't fill a Smarty. And as for that teapot next door to you. Who in their right mind gives a dog two names? If brains were elastic that fellow wouldn't stretch a wren's garter.'

It's always the same things she says. Always the same people she says things about. I like listening to her. She has one green eye and one brown eye and when she's talking to me I never know which one to look at. They are sad eyes and it makes me notice that everyone else has eyes sad too. At least when I look into them they are.

I don't know what has them so sad. They all live right beside the water. And Peter Corless owns a row boat. The river flows into the lake and Peter rows his boat out onto the lake to fish. He brings Arthur Guinness with him.

'Why do you call your dog Arthur Guinness?' I ask him and Peter starts looking around him, making sure the coast is clear before he reveals his secret.

'It's his idea,' Peter whispers, covering the side of his mouth with one hand and pointing down to Arthur Guinness with the other. 'In case either of us forgets. This way, between the two of us we'll always get it right.'

Just like Mother and me, I think to myself. 'It's me and you against the big bad world,' she says, snuggling me up against her at night before we go to sleep. 'Between the two of us we're a match for anyone.'

Mother's baking cupboard is a match for the big bad world too. It takes up one full wall in the kitchen. And it's as high as the ceiling. But this still isn't enough space for her. By the time I get back from the Riverside, Mother's baking is all over the kitchen. Sponge cakes, hot-cross buns, strawberry jams, apple tarts, rhubarb crumbles. And sherry trifle.

Sherry trifle is my favourite. Mother makes sherry trifle on special occasions. 'It's Bastille Day,' she announces, holding up her cutting knife like a sword. 'The anniversary of the French Revolution. Let them eat cake, Marie Antoinette said. Then they loped off her head. Whack! Just like that.' And she scalps a layer of cream off the trifle. Another day she bakes a cake in memory of her favourite saint. 'On this day they burned Joan of Arc. They tied her to a stake and said she was a witch. Five sizzling minutes later she was toast. This sherry trifle is for her memory.' And she holds up the trifle to the photograph of Saint Joan taped to the kitchen door. Other times the cake is for a dead princess gunned down in cold blood or a prisoner locked away in a cell for something she didn't do. There are so many occasions she runs out of sherry. Then she uses gin. But it's not the same when she uses gin, so I make sure there is always lots of sherry.

Her favourite occasion is the anniversary of Queen Maeve's death. 'Maeve was slain by her own kinsmen,' she tells me, removing Maeve's trifle from the oven. 'She rode into battle in her open cart and they gutted her. I'm descended from Queen Maeve. Which means you are too. We have royal blood. Don't ever forget that.' Then she licks the fingers she has just poked into Maeve's trifle.

Other times she has a special occasion just because she feels like it. 'It is the first Tuesday of the week,' she announces. 'This is my delicious Tuesday cake.'

'How many cakes have you baked?' I ask her.

'One thousand nine hundred and ninety-nine,' she replies. 'Not counting this one. That's an average of one a year since they nailed that man to the cross. But he had it coming.'

Every time she bakes she makes a big mess. Her cooking table is littered with spilled cartons of sugar and overturned jars of baking powder. Blobs of custard fly onto the walls and ceiling. Gouts of jam stain her clothes. She slides around the buttery floor with her oven trays. Humming away to Nina Simone on her stereo. *My baby don't care for shows. My baby don't care for clothes. My baby just cares for me.* It's a miracle she doesn't go belly-up. 'I won't fall,' she says as though she is reading my mind. 'I know my centre of gravity.' She never even wears the apron I bought for her birthday. It gets so bad I put on the apron myself and tidy up.

'It's good to make a mess,' she laughs, watching me tie on the apron. But I know she is only joking with me. 'You're my boy,' she says, when the kitchen is as good as new again. 'You're the best in the world. What would I do without you?'

'I'll never leave you,' I tell her.

'I know you won't,' she replies. 'It's just you and me against the big bad world.' And she smothers me with kisses, plunges her knife and cuts us both huge hunks of sherry trifle.

Night time is her favourite time for baking. 'It gets me through the dark hours,' she says, turning up Nina. 'Through the gin-house blues.' She stays up baking until the cock crows. The oven hums as Mother mixes her ingredients. Nina pours her heart out. I'm too tired to stay up this long but I ask her to wake me in the night so that I can come down and help her. The following day she says she came and woke me but I can't remember whether she did or not.

Sometimes I'm awake when I hear her come to bed. She looks in on me and I quickly sleep again. Sometimes I'm awake because of the nightmares and I go into her room to sleep. 'What are the nightmares about?' I ask her the next day. But it's too late by then.

Come morning Mother lies in. She loves her bed. And loves spending time in her room. One good thing about the nightmares is that I get to spend time in the room with her. But I wouldn't like it if I was there on my own. It's darker and smaller than my room. There is no closet to hang her dresses. Her books are scattered around the floor. Along with her creams and lotions and body sprays. All she has is a rickety cabinet with three wonky drawers and a cracked mirror. Her things spill out of the drawers. Pants and t-shirts. Skirts and jumpers. Stockings and underwear. When I look in the cracked mirror there is a ripple across my face. It's as though I'm looking in the water and it makes the room smaller again.

'It's a good job you don't need to bake in this room,' I tell her and she laughs.

While she has a lie-in I go shopping. She writes out a list of ingredients for her next baking mission and I have great fun hunting down everything she needs. Icing sugar. Chopped chocolate. Cocoa powder. Double cream. Caramel. I also buy fruit and vegetables; bread and cereal; some potatoes and meat for dinner. But we hardly ever make dinner and I throw them out again. Then I bring her breakfast in bed. I tear the skin off two mandarins and divide them into segments; peel some kiwi fruit and cut them into discs. I make her a cup of tea, two slices of toast and a bowl of muesli. I put it all on a tray and carry it upstairs. It's late in the day for breakfast but she doesn't mind. She knows I love making it for her. 'Are there any meringues?' she asks me, slurping her tea. I always forget something.

In my room I pick new countries from my atlas and learn capitals. Caracas. Pyongyang. Mogadishu. The Angel Falls is the highest waterfall. Mount Kilimanjaro is nineteen thousand three hundred and forty feet tall. The Orinoco is one thousand four hundred ninety seven and a half miles long.

'It's important to know these far away places,' Mother tells me when I go to her. 'One day you may have to take the long way home. Back to your centre of gravity. Your knowledge will keep you in the right direction.' Then she shows me a map of where we live. 'Look, here is the river. And look. You can see where it flows into the lake. And look. See that little dot right in the middle of the water. That's the lake-isle. That is *your* centre of gravity. Your river. Your rock. Your tree.' This is my favourite time of all, the two of us lying on her bed together, flicking through maps, sharing knowledge.

That night she wakes up screaming. Usually I get to her before the screaming but not this night. The screaming fades when I get up but I can still hear something. I tiptoe towards Mother's room to see if she's in bed. Already I can hear her. She is calling out a name, not mine. 'Clement,' I hear her say. She says it like she is in pain. Or a bit upset. 'Clement,' she calls out again. I turn the knob on her door and push it in. Then her voice changes. 'Get out,' she shouts. 'Get away from me. Stay away.'

I jump back out of the room and return to my bed. Her scratchy voice is still inside me and I hear the name again. Then I reach for my atlas. There are thirteen countries in South America, I tell myself. Brazil is the largest. Surinam is the smallest. Santiago is the capital of Chile. La Paz is the highest capital in the world. La Paz. It's Spanish. It means peace. Peace.

I hardly see Mother next day. I sit at the top of the stairs. Her door is closed and I can't hear anything. I have no idea what time of day it is. Early morning. Late afternoon. The middle of the night. Once or twice I hear some words. *Don't let me go. Promise me.* Then the stereo starts up. And Nina's voice sounds from her room.

Downstairs I find a pair of Marigold gloves under the sink and get busy. I run the Hoover over the hairy carpet. Suck up every bit of dirt in the corners. I dust down the telephone in the sitting room. Scrub the oven. Fill the coal bucket. I polish. Do the washing. Some more shopping. I rearrange the baking cupboard. The place looks as good as new.

When I've done the cleaning I go up the Riverside.

'Mastermind, come over here and settle a bet,' Fintan Power shouts over to me. He's standing at the door of his hotel. He's with a bunch of giggling girls.

'Ok girls,' he says with a flourish when I saunter over. 'This man has the last word. Mastermind, share some of your knowledge with my new friends from Tennessee. Countries in Africa or states in America. Which has more?'

'Neither,' I say.

'What do you mean neither?'

'Fifty countries. Fifty states,' I say and walk off.

I see Peter Corless and Arthur Guinness.

'How about a turn on the lake, Mastermind?' he calls to me.

He dips his oars in the black water and pulls. Soon he lets me hold an oar. It's so heavy I tilt over to one side, face to face with the lapping water. I stare into it. The water ripples and in it I see my reflection. Like the mirror in Mother's room. Except now it looks like a way older version of myself. Soon I get used to the oar and Peter lets me try with the other one. And then both at the same time.

'Just like swimming,' he says and pats Arthur Guinness.

We row through the narrow river channel. Tall leafy trees pack together along the riverbanks. Lily pods float on the surface. Reeds grow out of the water's edge. Clouds of midges swirl in the summer light. A loon dives. Arthur Guinness barks at the splash. The river channel widens and the lake water spreads out before us. It's breezier now, and Peter takes the oars. The water rocks the boat. The wind twists my eyes and they glisten over. In front of me I see a cluster of trees and rocks growing right out of the water. They almost reach the sky.

'Gallagher's Island,' Peter says, drawing up the oars and letting them rest in their hooks.

We glide through the water, towards the island. Water laps against the boat. Apart from that it is silent.

'Who's Gallagher?' I ask.

'Gallagher didn't like people. So he came out here to live,' Peter says. 'But I don't know how anyone could live out here. It's a fickle place.'

Then he just hunches forward, leans on the oars, and stares out at the island trees.

'No man is an island,' he says, 'even if he wants to be.'

Peter draws the oars and lets the current take us to the shore. With one of the oars he guides the boat to the strip of sand. I slide up over the bow and splash in the water. I feel stones prick my feet. Then it's sandy. Peter drags in the boat and Arthur Guinness leaps onto the sand. I race up the shore, as far as the grassy bank. I pause and gaze up at the trees and rocks. Peter waves me on. I wander into the trees.

Twigs snap where I walk and flimsy leaves rustle above me. I find a crumbling brick house. It's not much bigger than a shed. The roof has caved in and through the rubble nettles peak out and wave. Clumps of moss stick to the brittle walls. Tangled tree roots emerge out of the ground because they have no place else to go.

I climb the hill. I can see the entire lake now. The mountain rising over it. Clouds hovering. I see Peter near the water's edge, feeding Arthur Guinness from his hand. It's like one of Mother's special occasions. I call out to them but they don't hear me. I call out to Mother. I think of all the times I go to her in her nightmares. Run my hands through strands of her hair. Claw at the dark spaces separating us. I try to think what it was like being Gallagher. What he looked like. What he had to eat out here. What he did during the day. Maybe he thought he was in a faraway place. Maybe he came out here to forget. Or to remember. Like I do when I'm up the Riverside. It's like an extinct world. The centre of the universe. The last great hiding place.

I think of what Mother said when she showed me the map. *Your river. Your rock. Your tree.* I think this is where I want to be, at the top of this hill. At the very top. Where Nessa Flynn says I belong. I could sleep close to the stars with nothing to wake me except the wind. And I could remember and forget everything.

'Are you up for a spot of fishing?' Peter asks me when we're in the boat again.

He hooks a worm and casts off. The wind picks up. The boat rocks. He reels in and the rod bends.

'What is it?' I ask. 'Have you caught something?'

'It's a perch,' he says. 'Not bad, eh. On my first cast off. Here. Feel how slippery it is.'

It's gets windier. The sky darkens. The boat lurches from side to side. Peter casts off again. And lands another perch.

'This is the spot,' he says.

The water is high and black. I grab an oar and peer into the water. I can see the face again. The older face. Stern with black eyes. The blackest eyes I've ever seen. They sneer at me through the broken waves. Behind me Peter says something and the face smirks. I stab at it with the oar and it smirks some more. Peter calls out to me again. What is the deepest lake in the world? I shout back. Where is the source of the Nile? I swing around with my oar as he roars at me one final time.

My hands are blistered when we get back but I don't care. I can't wait to tell Mother about my adventure. She's in the kitchen, standing by her cooking table. Sitting at the table is a man I've never seen.

'Billy, this is Clement,' she says and the man offers out his hand.

'Where did you come from?' I ask. 'No one comes to our house.'

'I'm a friend of your mother's. A new friend.'

'Mother doesn't have friends. Is this the man you call out to in the middle of the night?' I ask without looking at him.

Mother looks down at the floor.

'How many cakes are you baking today?' I ask.

'I better go,' says the man.

'No. You don't have to go,' says Mother. 'He has to get used to this. He can choose the easy way or the hard way.'

'Get used to what?'

'Clement has been to Egypt.'

'How many countries are there in Africa?' I ask.

'Billy!'

'What is the deepest lake in the world?'

'What, eh. I'm afraid you have me there, young man.'

'Billy! Stop this. Now!'

'Where is Byzantium?'

'Billy. Get upstairs. NOW.'

Upstairs I write down the answers in my notebook. Make lists of foreign words from my phrase books. *Auf Wiedersehen. Hasta la Vista. Sayonara. Ciao.* I lie on my bed and think of the swan's graceful flight. I see the perch Peter Corless caught. I wonder about the face I saw in the water. Then I hear them come upstairs. They whisper outside my door. Mother is talking.

'Billy, can we come in. Clement wants to take us out for a meal. He says you can have whatever you want. It'll be fun, Billy. Think of all the nice desserts on the menu. Come on Billy. We can make it a very special occasion.'

Then he starts into this very special occasion talk too. Telling me about future special occasions to look forward to. As though we're having a great time together all the time. As though we've known each other all our lives. Now he's taking me out on the water. Going to show me how to fish. We can camp on the island, he says. Just me and him. Who does he think we are? Robinson Crusoe and Man Friday, I suppose. That's a good one. He didn't even know the answer to my questions. Easy questions. I clutch my notebook and get ready to ask him some more. But he doesn't hang around for my quiz. He knows Mother will see him for the teapot he is. Just like everyone else with not enough brains to fill a Smarty. I hear them go into Mother's room. They giggle like the Tennessee girls. Then Nina starts to sing.

I pound downstairs as loudly as I can. I go into the kitchen. I open the baking cupboard. Pour out the bag of flour. Sprinkle sugar and spices on the floor. Smear honey on the walls. In the fridge rests the largest sherry trifle I've seen yet. 'What's the special occasion?' I wonder aloud and plunge my face into it. I shake away blobs of jelly and rub them over her precious Saint. I pour cream through her wash. Plop dollops of custard on the telephone that never rings.

'It's good to make a mess,' I laugh and check the cupboard one last time – to make sure I haven't missed any ingredients. My hands find Mother's ginger jar. It's sticky at the back of the cupboard and I have to yank it out. A biscuit tin comes with it, and spills open onto the floor. Photographs and letters and pieces of paper spill across the floor. They land among clumps of jelly and melting ice-cream. One of the photographs lands face up. It's black and white. A man standing. A baby in his arms. His black eyes make him look very stern. The baby has huge eyes. Black eyes. *The blackest eyes I've ever seen.* As I reach for the cutting knife the room begins to sway.

The boat rocks. The sky darkens. The breeze carries me towards the shore. From the bedroom Nina's words sound. *My baby don't care for shows. My baby don't care for clothes. My baby just cares for me.* I see Mother standing by the rocks and I wave. She waves back and starts laughing when she sees the mess on my face. Suddenly she screams. 'Clement. Oh, Clement.'

'It's just you and me, baby,' I whisper. 'Just you and me against the big bad world.'

I hear lake water lapping.

Lap Dancing

ventually, as I knew would happen, we get around to talking about women. We don't know a lot about them, Jules and I, but every time we meet up Jules says we should try to chat about things we know nothing about. The other day, for example, we had a conversation about lap-dancing clubs. In spite of many protests, one has opened up a few doors down from where Jules lives. Jules has no problem with the dancing girls – after all, they have bills to pay like the rest of us. He is just dismayed that they have chosen to take over what was his favourite pub. 'I used to drink there all the time,' he keeps saying to me. Now all he wants to do is sip coffee and protest.

'Jules,' I plead with him, 'the pub is gone and it's not coming back. It's time to move on. There are other pubs.'

But it's like talking to a stone.

In fact I'm surprised at how far Jules is taking his protest. After our conversation about lap-dancing clubs, he went to Penney's and bought several white sheets. He then bought a tin of red paint, a bristly brush and painted a slogan - *GIVE US BACK OUR PUB*. He pierced the sheets with holes and put a lath across the bottom. 'I hear that stops them blowing all over the place,' he said. Then he hung the sheets outside his upstairs windows. He called around to his neighbours and gave them sheets. 'We need to form a human chain,' he said to anyone who would listen. 'We must bring the street to a standstill. Let these guys know what we think of their seedy plans.'

Usually, I'm as willing as the next man to follow a worthy cause, but I wondered is it not a little late in the day for all this? After all, the new owners have already moved in, held auditions and plastered posters of tempting dancers across the windows of their new club. But, as I say, Jules doesn't want to know.

The new owners are among the first to notice Jules' sheets, which, in spite of all the holes, are flapping passionately about and wrapping themselves up in twists - so much so that the slogan is illegible. Nevertheless, the new owners feel urged to approach Jules.

To encourage him to simmer down about their seedy plans, they promise Jules free admission to the club for the first three months. Every hour, they put exotic fliers in his letterbox, tease him with slogans of their own and ply him with photographs of popular dancers – a different dancer for each night of the week, according to Jules. They even hint that there might be a private audience in it for him when he storms down there to tell them precisely what they can do with their 'brochures.' 'Come inside. Take a look around,' a guy wearing shades says to him.

But Jules remains determined never to set foot inside the place – not after what they've done to it. I feel a bit sorry for him, especially after all the effort he has gone to with the red paint and sheets full of holes. To rub salt into his wounds, it's also becoming apparent that his protest has actually attracted people to the dancing club – that is, if the lengthy queues every night are anything to go by.

'No wonder they're keen to throw you freebies,' I say when we next meet up.

'I've a good mind to torch the place,' he says, gulping a mouthful of coffee.

'And where will that get you?' I ask.

'Things just aren't the same,' he laments.

'Have you ever met a lap-dancer?' I ask him, hoping to steer our conversation in a more interesting direction.

'No, but once I had a conversation with a masseuse,' he replies, and I see my plan is working.

Because I know Jules has wanted to have a chat about women for a long time. He doesn't have one himself but he thinks the world of them. Every time he sees one he says something charming. Or at least he thinks he does. Either way, he claims he always means well. 'I want them to feel good about themselves,' he says, 'so why wouldn't I say something charming?'

Take what is a typical day for him – at least until this lap-dancing business began. What should amount to no more than a straightforward stroll to the old sweet shop for his paper always becomes an epic voyage of discovery. En route, if he sees a girl shopping indecisively for a new blouse, he quickly forgets about his paper, saunters into the shop and tells the girl that the blouse looks great on her, that it really suits her milky

complexion or draws out her mermaid eyes. It doesn't end
there. When he enters a shop with queues he deliberately joins
the longest queue because it contains more girls. 'We're having
a lot of weather lately,' he announces to the queue. 'Can you
believe it's only four months to Christmas,' he muses, shaking
his baffled head. 'What is your favourite film?' he might ask the
girl standing closest to him.

This forbearing attitude involves him in all sorts of delays.
Not so long ago, he spent an afternoon buying a Prize Bond in
the Post Office. 'Today, I talked to a girl from Tanzania,' he said
by way of explanation, when he finally showed up to meet me.
As a matter of fact, it was the last time we were to meet up in his
beloved pub. And all Jules could talk about was this girl from
Tanzania. 'She had unspeakably beautiful eyes,' he continued
and I gave him a funny look because it's not often he is stuck for
words. 'You know, Jim,' he added, huddling up to me in the
dark-lit atmosphere he had come to love so much, 'there just
isn't enough time. I wish there was a bit of me everywhere.'

No doubt, this helps explain why I often find him chatting
away to the girl at the Credit Union's foreign exchange desk. He
doesn't have any Dollars or Pesos of his own to convert but he
likes saying hello to the various nationalities that pass through.
It's also a good place to witness him listen – one thing he doesn't
do a lot of. Of course, he hasn't got a clue what anyone is saying
and I find it strange that the only people he listens to are those
he cannot understand. But he says he likes the sounds of all the
foreign words. 'They're comforting,' he says.

The opening of the lap-dancing club, however, has changed
things. Post Office afternoons are just not the same. He has been

on the receiving end of funny looks in the Credit Union. His morning strolls no longer coax easy smiles, delicate grins or lingering clinks of admiration.

'I'm not hitting the right notes,' he tells me.

So I tag along to see if there is anything different in his approach.

In the morning, upon complimenting a girl's mobile phone ring-tone, she glares at him and says *get a grip*. Later, in a hair salon, when he asks a lady what she thinks of his hairstyle, she suggests he keep it short – the conversation and the hair. But the last nail in the coffin arrives when he offers to help an old lady cross a busy road and she goes for him with her handbag. 'I'm a married woman, you pervert,' she says and lets him have it.

'Where is it going wrong?' he asks me in the coffee shop and I'm stuck for an answer.

It's as if part of him has disappeared – along with his favourite pub. Yet when I put this to him, Jules refuses to accept that the arrival of lap-dancing on his doorstep is a factor. And when I gently rile him, he's adamant it's not down to his faltering charm. Then he waves me closer to him, into one of his familiar huddles.

'It's women,' he whispers to me, blowing the froth off his creamy coffee. 'They're changing.'

'How do you mean?' I ask.

'For one thing they have plumper lips.'

'OK, but I can't say I've noticed.'

'And I'm pretty sure they can now go invisible. Yesterday, a man was jailed for stealing anti-wrinkle cream. I was into the court to see for myself. During cross-examination he said the cream was for his girlfriend. But she was nowhere to be seen.'

In truth, I think Jules' past is starting to catch up with him. Shortly after he walked out on his employer, Jules began life as a handyman. Every Thursday, he puts an ad in the paper saying he can tidy neglected lawns, patio unwanted gardens, put caps on chirping chimneys. That sort of thing. He also lays claims to being quite good with a hedge strimmer and in possession of an uncanny knack for hanging doors and fitting side gates. After a brief plunge into the world of pianos, he is even well on his way to convincing a rich spinster he is the man to tune the baby-grand Steinway for which she desperately seeks an expert. Now all that remains is for him to convince her black wolfhound.

Black wolfhounds aside, for a long time he received the benefit of doubt. But gradually people have to come to realise that Jules isn't quite what he says he is. In a quiet moment, Jules is the first to admit he's a bit of a chancer. Sometimes, in fact, he is way too hard on himself, and I'm quick to remind him he's human like the rest of us. As usual, there's no talking to him.

'They must be on to me,' he concludes sadly.

Several days pass before we meet up again. Through the grapevine, I've heard that Jules is keeping to himself. Especially, after only one other person showed up to form a link in his human chain. So I'm a little anxious myself – as it completely slipped my mind. Nevertheless, he is very excited.

'I met one of them,' he tells me.

'Who?'

'A lap-dancer. *Do you think I am any good?* she asked me.'

'Did you go?'

'I did not. I was moping around there, trying to think up

another protest. Then I stepped into the old sweet shop for a Mars bar. That's where I met Veronica. She was on a break and thought I'd been to her performance. Think again, I said to her. Then she told me the sweet shop is closing and a casino is opening – right across the road from the lap-dancing club.'

'I suppose the war paint and holy sheets will be on display again,' I say.

'Christ no,' he booms, throwing an Espresso into him. 'This casino sounds like a great place. I really like the idea of a midnight game of cards. It beats playing Old Maid at home and listening to those useless sheets.'

'What about the old sweet shop?'

'A sweet tooth will only get you so far. Besides, that place never stocks Mars bars.'

'I didn't know you could play cards.'

'Veronica showed me. Rumour has it there'll be free coffee for poker players. I can't wait. Veronica says as soon as it's up and going, she's going to hang up her thong and become a croupier. She promises me the occasional good card. So I told her I'd see her there, and do you know what she said? *I like a man who is willing to take a risk.*'

Sun Showers

Every time Naylor does not see eye to eye with the world he blames progress. When he doesn't sleep at night, it's because he hears the internet dial-up singing in his ears. When he walked away from his job, it was because he could no longer listen to his boss say 'let's do lunch.' When he gets lost staggering home from his favourite pub he blames it entirely on new roads. 'Things better stop changing,' he can be heard muttering to the Moon.

Now matters have taken a turn for the worse. It comes in the guise of the latest new road, a vital addition to the city's wrangle of thoroughfares. It is the only way forward, planners announce, as the diggers roll up to their marks. On this occasion the only way forward happens to be through Naylor's front room.

'What's wrong with him,' I say to Nikki, Naylor's long suffering girlfriend. 'He's only lived in that house for two minutes.'

'That's neither here nor there,' Nikki sighs. 'This time the world has wounded him forever. Talk to him. I've given up.'

I quickly discover there is something in what Nikki says. In small ways Naylor is already fastening down the hatches against the world that has hurt him. He has stopped shopping at Tesco because they keep rearranging the shelves. He no longer answers his phone to numbers he does not recognise. He's avoiding contact with doctors after a GP promised to map out his medical destiny. He has become an avid collector of travel articles out of the Sunday magazines. But he doesn't go anywhere. He won't even step beyond his front door.

'What's the point?' he pleads when, at last, he answers one of my calls. 'It's impossible to get anywhere. The lights are always red. As soon as I get halfway through the roundabout the lane disappears. And, it's always raining. Even when the sun is out. I'm fed up with all these sun showers. The disruption to my life is complete.'

'So what are you going to do?' I ask. 'Become a recluse?'

'That's a great idea,' he bellows. 'As of today I'm taking a vow of solitude. You can call me, but not between one and four. Channel4's top fifty musicals of all time begin this afternoon and I don't want anybody interfering. It's just about the only pleasurable thing left for me.'

'And where does Nikki fit into this solitary attitude?'

'Women are good things but not at this moment,' he replies. Then he hangs up.

'You're right,' I tell Nikki, setting down my phone. 'He's a victim again.'

No sooner have I delivered this ominous verdict than Nikki is sobbing uncontrollably. Looking at her makes me wonder how she held out this long. Her hair is a scrambled yellow mess, clumps of mascara spring from her waterlogged eyes, she wears an expression from which there is no escape.

'I did one last shop for him,' she blubbers through it all, making no attempt to curtail her misery. 'I wish I knew how to help him down off his cross,' she sobs.

'Stay here as long as you want,' I offer, and warn her about my sleepwalking.

Whereupon she produces a bottle of Jack Daniels, plonks herself in front of my television and switches on Channel4.

Despite the best efforts of Nikki and Channel4's top fifty musical season, Naylor has been up on the cross a long time. So long, in fact, that few remember when or how it all began. Personally, I suspect his martyrdom has its origins in the time a planner placed Naylor's application to build at the bottom of the slush pile. Not one to beat about the bush, at once Naylor called the planner an ape and later presented to his nemesis a box of bananas and nuts. 'These are for you, ape-man,' he said to the planner, who had no idea what to make of the gifts laid out before him. Some time later again, Naylor's then girlfriend fell for the planner, and a punch to the face accompanied the next box of bananas and nuts. 'You do not appear remorseful,' the judge said to him when the case came before the courts. 'Neither does the gorilla,' Naylor replied.

It was the ensuing week spent in Castlerea Prison that first alerted Naylor to the therapeutic effects of *West Side Story* and *Mary Poppins*. Upon his release he made a bee-line for the nearest Xtra-vision, and rented every musical he could lay his hands on. Behind the Xtra-vision counter, a fervent member of a local dramatics group was smitten by the sensitive felon's taste in movies. There and then, Nikki took it upon herself to assist Naylor's restoration into society, and, for a long time seemed to possess in her delicate fingertips precisely what magic was required. Until this latest episode, that is, when her restorative powers abruptly evaporated.

'Flynn, let me ask you a question,' he growls the next time I call. 'Where are all these roads going? How long is it going to take to get there? Why does there have to be so much noise? Don't call me again until you have answers. *Showboat* is on this afternoon. It's the only pleasure left to me.'

'It's as though he has given up on life,' Nikki sighs, pouring herself a large whiskey.

'Every day is doomsday for Naylor,' I concede, helping myself to a drink as well.

'He's just so sensitive, Michael. I've never seen anybody to suffer so from contact with people. It's what draws me to him. Where will this road take us, I wonder?'

'He asked me the same thing and then hung up.'

'To forgetting,' she says, hoisting her glass.

'To remembering,' I say, clinking.

To rid her tearful complexion of this unhappy time and some lingering globs of mascara, Nikki books herself into a beauty parlour. Meantime, I take a stroll as far as Naylor's Road – the name Nikki and I have chosen for the important new route-way. There are lots of jeeps, dumper trucks, and diggers standing by. Men work the ground with picks. They sing as they work. Other men stand back-to-back with mobile traffic lights showing red. Between them stretches a temporary driving lane. However, just like on the roundabout, the lane quickly disappears. The disappearing lane confuses people. One minute there is a road. The next minute there isn't. Many stop driving altogether. But it doesn't matter because the lights remain red. An atmosphere of intolerance kicks in. Car-horns flare. People shake violent fists. 'This is the way of new roads,' a workman tells disbelieving traffic makers, as though they should know better. And it begins to rain.

'I know this tragedy,' Nikki confesses, when we meet up back at my place.

She is sitting with her bottle of Jack, flicking through a homeopathy brochure.

'So what if the roads are disorganised,' she says, sipping from her glass. 'One day they will be beautiful again. Maybe they are already. Beauty doesn't belong only in the past or in the future.'

At once, these heartfelt words grab my attention and it strikes me that I could apply them to Nikki herself. She may have unmanageable hair but it's obvious that her visit to the beauty parlour is paying off. Her eyelashes curl out invitingly. Her lips have acquired a glistening hue. Simultaneously, she can now offer tragic words and withhold tears.

Thinking about Nikki helps take my mind off Naylor's Road. Awake in my bed, an incommunicable longing reaches out to me. 'Save me, Anthony,' she pleads into the unheeding night. 'Save me from these tragic flaws.' This night opera worries me. Further cause for concern is my sleepwalking. It took me through the third floor window of a London tenement when Naylor and I worked there on the sites. Naylor witnessed the entire thing. He was outside the tenement, waltzing a traffic cone around a squad car full of angry policemen. I landed on the roof of the squad car, and, for the next twelve months, couldn't walk or sleep properly. I still don't sleep properly. And my sense of direction remains erratic. Amidst the indefinable territories of night I am liable to end up anywhere.

'She's talking in her sleep,' I tell Naylor. 'Some guy called Anthony.'

'The devil take her,' he hisses across the phone-line. 'Tell me about the road. How fast are the men digging?'

'They're progressing at a steady pace,' I say. 'You should come down for a look. They sing as they dig. They sing very well.'

'To hell with all the singing. I can't hear any singing.'

'Not with the internet dial-up buzzing in your ears, you can't,' I remind him, but he has already put the phone down.

'I once suggested he sign up for the broadband,' Nikki reflects into her whiskey. 'It's so much easier on the soul.'

And so it is. Nikki pines for her suffering man, Naylor shuts out the troublesome world, and I find myself sleepwalking through the flawed traffic lights where a midnight band of men pick their way through the tortured earth. All the time singing as they dig. Mournfully in the rain.

'It's the road,' Nikki says, when I tell her about my wayward hours. 'The road puts you in this mood because you're missing your friend.'

'He used to be the best company.'

'How do you think I feel?' she replies, knocking back her drink. 'It's not everyday I swallow bottles of whiskey and spend afternoons in beauty salons.'

'What is it today? A body peel? A honey rub?'

'A Cleopatra bath,' she says. 'I think I'll bring the bourbon along.'

'A Cleopatra bath,' I tell Naylor. 'What do you think of that?'

'The devil take her,' he grumbles.

'She looks very provocative.'

'Don't talk to me about provocation,' he says and hangs up.

Is it all a ruse, I wonder? Behaving like a recluse. Avoiding work. Getting lost. As though these petulant acts of defiance will somehow whisk Naylor away from a place he no longer recognises. From a place he has no wish to belong. Within the gathering darkness I can see the three of us standing by the new road, listening to the dig's mournful ceremonies. Unflappable Nikki; reclusive Naylor; and myself, perpetually lost and confused. There is no foundation to the road, no end in sight. And all the time, they're digging. Digging and singing. A plaintive melody, at once tragic and beautiful.

'The night wanderer returns,' Nikki announces, when I blunder my way into the spare room.

She's sitting in front of a mirror, applying a crimson blusher to her morning face. I park myself beside her.

'You're right,' I say, resting my weary head upon her shoulder. 'The road has put a spell on me.'

'Naylor used to have a road like it,' she replies, reaching an arm about me. 'Only he hasn't been able to find it recently. He says it contains everything he desires.'

'I wonder what that could be.'

'That's what I asked him. But he just tapped his finger off his nose, winked at me and said to ask you.'

Outside, thunder clouds bully their way across the morning sky and try their best to interrupt our lonely moments. Soon the sun showers begin. Nikki reaches for the bottle and pours two glasses of Jack.

'Here's to Naylor,' I toast, winking at her through the mirror.

'To Naylor,' she whispers and winks back.

We sit there in the silence and gradually they reach us. The sounds of picks going at the earth, and the low tunes of men singing in the rain. Occasionally there is a collective sigh, heavy and prolonged, that seems to draw from deep inside the earth itself and call attention to a moment of passing beauty. A last glimpse of sunlight before clouds, perhaps.

Late Night Coffee Bar: 28th March 2004

Saturday night into Sunday morning. Near close. Twenty minutes give or take. Calls for last coffees. Final detonations of sulphur. Chastening whorls of smoke.

Tonight, endangered species abound. Soon-to-be hard-to-find sorts. They have shunned all announcements; hidden from its arrival; fabricated forgotten ideals. They feel gypped. Cut loose. Unacknowledged in the scheme of things.

At your peril you mention it. Hairs bristle. Lips bloat and curl. Daggers spool from suddenly lustrous eyes. If you must talk of it cover your mouth; elbow and wink; whisper the little word. This soft café light is no place now or ever for these struck-off amber glints.

Hear their mild rebellions. *Say it isn't true.* Their wistful pleas. *Where will we go?* Talk of their lot to be. *Things just won't be the same.*

Chiselling declamations from a talky kind of singer don't help this end-is-nigh mood. His long throaty lines jostle for a hitch in the smoke-turning room. Piano trickles along. Muted trumpet braves the singer's forlorn gist. Like a clapped-out elephant alone in the bush desert night. And the voice seeps unrelenting through the smoky vibe and unfurling layers of imperceptible static.

Amidst these woe-begone moments here I am. Taking a sip. Stealing my moment. Unlikely suspirations one and all.

Our waitress prepares herself; folds an apron; eyes the clock. Almost there. Nearly done. The unflappable second hand does its bit. But the vital sign labours. At odds with her onwards yearning, it teases out the closing moment. Prolonging the end with a faltering rhythm. Is it a trick of the light? A test of her wavering dedication? Has this rueful band of smokers cast a spell? A charlatan aspect that possesses the minute hand. Haltingly to the hour mark. Only then can she flee.

Forget about it. Avert those restless eyes elsewhere. Wash some cups. Clear another table. Bequeath a refill to your favourites. You might never see them again.

A shot for the balcony-eyed sergeant alone in the corner. What will his trembling yellow fingers do? He's on duty tonight. The graveyard shift. Hanging out in the quiet side before the move up town. Before silly time. And he must push himself between six-day-fasting-frenzied youths trying to rip one another's heart out. To uphold a blood-soaked prestige. And the pride of a ramshackle cause.

Two steaming mugs for a grouty pair beneath the bookshelf wall. Company for the pouch of Golden Virginia and Rizla rolls they work with meticulous zest. Super-sizing to mark the occasion.

A glass with a handle for the slip-of-a-thing at the window. On a high stool. Right next to me. Hidden for the most part behind the steadily turning pages of a graphic novel. In between deft flicks of a done-and-dusted page her cigarette arm protrudes like an elegant spout. And busy eyes scroll up and down the intricate designs of the picture tale. Its title is concealed, like a hologram, within the outstretched arms of a green-bandage cadaver that walks towards a frothing ghoul rising from the bubbling muds. Bleeding black letters on the back cover spell out instantaneous perils of forgoing next month's issue.

At the table below me three wanderers. Two guys and a girl. Backpacks that have brought the elephant to its knees. Stitched on revelations. *Cats have got nine lives but you've only got one. I love to travel, but hate to arrive. In the potholes is where it's at.* Between artificial puffs of a leaded pencil, the girl blathers like there's no tomorrow. She could talk for her country and soon makes the discovery. 'I'm a very oral person,' she announces and, dragging heavily on her pencil, a tacked-on corollary spells it out a little more: 'I always have to have something in my mouth.'

She launches a tablet of gum, lays down the pencil, tilts her head and traps the returning pill between her teeth. Then gnashes into her prize.

Abetted by a folding map, the other two plot a way out.

As a boy I harboured dreams of travel. I turned atlas pages. Memorised capital cities. Pined for strange horizons. Paramaribo. Gantok. Ouagadougou. Geography was my subject. Each moment became a lesson. Every game revealed my wish. I wanted to hike across a continent. Say hi in every language. Become infatuated with a sallow skinned girl. It was all very exotic. I made secret promises. Immersed myself in complicated sagas. Tried to giddyup the time. And when it came I couldn't move.

Over the bookshelf monochrome mounts depict cities by night. Three dark-towns of gloom. Cityscapes oozing rue. In spite of it all the bookshelf sags into a smile, invading the space between the Rizla rollers, low-down in confidential bidding. The plot unfurls beneath the brooding city nights. A pantomime straight from the silver screen. Wise guy and flunkey. The brains of the intrigue. And the no-brains. Either side of a tinny ashtray. Rollies burning down.

Brains is busy. An index finger points to his ear and performs tiny orbits. While his other hand curls into a fist. And a torqued forearm follows through. As though someone must thrust well with a blade. What are they hatching? A weighty deed for the flunkey. A stand to the last ditch. The beginning of mad things.

Beneath a Chinese hat, a pair of rippling jowls presses against the window. The owner wobbles in; allows the hat fall back at his neck; where it's held by a string. He's had a few but carries it well. A content looking man. Recently retired perhaps. His health is rude. And people in his family live a long time. Maybe he just got out of the clink. Straight to the till with him. And to the waitress: 'I'd like a large pint of Guinness please.' Soft. Patient. Knowing. A poker face to bring down the house and a mien no girl wants to disappoint. A devil of a performer. 'Wait,' she says indulging for the moment the impish whim.

And she disappears out the back.

I used to drink in a bar at the end of this road. Along the narrow street; down an alley; a sawdust floor and cut-out keg pews. Low tables by the wall. A candle for the dim light. I used to bring a girl there. We talked about it all; forgot the time; drank the rent. We shielded our eyes when we left, skipped down to the pier and fed the swans. We tiptoed home across the bridge, told each other we'd stay awake forever and fell asleep to the sounds of clattering beer crates. When they shut it down I got drunk and said I'd open it again. It was something I really wanted to believe. A reluctance to let go, perhaps. And the romance of the unattainable.

Thereabouts, nowadays, a flurry of casino-neon lights up another fancy and the beefy doorman stands over the pot of gold. As for the girl - she won the lotto, packed her bags and ruined her dainty feet. At least that's what she tells me happens in her dreams.

No-brains stares at the talking head opposite him. All the time. In awe. As though it is full of wonders he lacks. Gusto and spleen. Attitude and can-do. Brains knows this. He oozes wisdom and his effervescence compels. Ferociously, he wags the pointing finger in his cohort's face. Conferring the plot's true essence. While sparring with a tortuous learner. No-brains hangs off every word, gesture and vibe. He wears an army-green brim hat ringed with a felt blue mantra: *I am a fucking paddy*. Metallic figurines dangle from the hat. A walking boot; a pistol; a loaded dice; and a long roofless car with fins. Vigorously, he nods his head at the wagging finger. Grateful to be a part in the deed. Inside the circle. Part of the shakedown.

Meanwhile the figurines tremble. Like death-watches. In the sticks of a kindling flame. Because they know.

A metal hiss floods the low-key room. Mucky spume sloshes through a rib-neck glass. The drinker ducks beneath his triangular crown. Caresses settle time along. Like a child at Christmas time. In thrall to the unexpected gift.

He lets our waitress in on his ruse.

'I don't know,' she replies. 'A little ghost out back tells me you're a serious-in-jest kind of guy.'

'It is a good looking drink.'

'I've heard tell it can put a chest on a man's hairs.'

'I don't suppose you've any onions.'

'My God, an onion eater to boot.'

'The breath drives the missus doo-lally.'

'I'm sure she wouldn't have you any other way.'

'She can be a force of nature.'

'And you're a terrible man. In cahoots with the wee hours of the night.'

'Do you like my hat?'

'That hat is definitely wrong.'

But he leaves it on anyway.

I have a four-year-old nephew who calls me Mr. Wrong. I can't remember how it started. He drew a picture of a house with crooked walls, oblong windows and an upside down door. The garden was full of weeds. The chimney was on fire. He said it was where I lived. He even drew a Mrs. Wrong – a stick insect with feet growing out of her head. She was in the kitchen, nibbling the instructions to a smoking Zanussi. I'm going to use him for bait the next time I go to the lake. Or maybe put him in a room with the terrible frog.

A guy with a sleeved guitar appears. The girl's eyes smile. 'What's happening?' he says, mimicking a fiend from her gory story.

But she is rescued by the chiming register. And the jingling coin basket. And the spluttering coffee machine that appears to have run out of steam.

Our waitress kills the music; draws the catch; holds the door. And it occurs to everyone: The minute hand has fallen into place.

The wanderers swing their packs towards the night, the sergeant is already gone. The large-pint-of-muck man doffs his hat, mulls over a gesture and crowns his latest queen. No-brains looks to Brains for a way to fend off the inevitable.

Two o'clock and ticking. Been a long day. Waitress wants home. To dress down. Unwind. Without sermon she turfs us out. But I don't mind. Time to move on. Face the world. Make some new mistakes. Contrive a misunderstanding. Hesitate. Speak at the bad time.

Which is why sometimes, once every now and again; on the occasion of a blue moon; at the unreasonable hour; in the time it takes to smoke one final cigarette; as the elephant's lonely trumpet seeks his ancestor's trail and the wanderer's soliloquy scatters through the valley silence, and the lines of the low tunes ripple slowly through the room like the spreading rings about a raindrop that touches the unmoving water, and silent epiphanies rush the seconds in between songs, and I really haven't very much to say, this is where I like to be. The other side of midnight. Saturday night into Sunday morning. At the quiet end. Where the meter doesn't tick as fast. When solace reigns and ghosts oblige. For twenty minutes. Or thereabouts. Before closing time.

I can taste the ocean now. The blue moon begins to turn again. Tonight, I think I'll walk home to my crooked house; stir my good lady from her wealthy dreams; sort out her crumpled feet; ask her what she wants to see; lace some walking boots; comment on the waning solstice; and tell her let's go.

Saturday Night At The Movies

On screen the shadow of a gunman. Tentative along a sweating wall. A shot rings out, suspending the silent black ballet. Another shot. Quickly then a third, fourth and fifth. A body slumps to the ground.

The camera changes course. Angles down. Closes in. Inexorably, as though inviting the audience to complete the bloody ordeal, it recovers the merest essentials of the gunman's gruesome fate - a redundant weapon, a dark-stain wrist, a limping pulse. An eerie violin darkens the slate a little more. Paving the way for the cause of it all.

Enter a pouting killer.

Shimmering through her smoking gun a payback glare. Ransom lips. And blackwater eyes that reveal what she truly is. Beauty to die for.

She leans close to her victim, enticing him with the ponderous scent of her tainted perfume. Forgiving to a fault, his valediction craves one last dance. But it is the death of him and, ridding the scene of painstakingly acquired dignity, the killer's lips lapse into an imperceptible smile.

The camera backs away. The orchestra flees. The silver screen shudders through a chilling finale. And to the gallery bequeaths a warm corpse and a frozen heart.

Elsewhere a quickly developing consequence. Paddywagon siren. The rap of a condemning gavel. A gallows plinth and a twisting rope. The hangman's knell.

And everyone has seen enough. The movie theatre brightens. The curtain skiffs across the film's climactic score. The projector begins to run out of time.

In the front row the old movie buff is already fumbling with another ending. Like many before him, he has fallen for these unlovable charms. He sees beyond her brutish urge and callous whims; clings to her language of deceit; longs for an instant of her time.

Briefly entering an epilogue, he conjures a passing dialogue. Reconstructs the crime. Engages an imagination run amok to deter the god-awful end decided for her. Tweaking a blurb he knows by heart, he defends with desperation this misunderstood girl.

Let's face it your honour, the guy had it coming. He was bad news, a vile thing, the lowest of the low.

Distractions garble his favourable reckonings. Rustlings of the quickly departing; gatherings of the no-nonsense usher; splutterings of the spent film reel.

By and by, the swirling dust settles. Keys jangle. The exit door beckons.

But his face remains an unresolved outcome. Awkward thinking knots his brow. Remaining in the dream a moment, he relocates to a distant lot; traces long forgotten lines, absurd twists in the plot. Face to face with pretend-exits from which he is forced to choose, nagging doubts try to splice the real and the impossible. Returning to the picture-house, a question lingers. Is there another way out?

He's held up in the foyer. To a captive audience, a talking superhero heralds groundbreaking virtues of a future presentation. Fluttering overhead, larger-than-life banners issue ultimatums to the world. Eventually the superhero becomes aware of the threat and, for a moment, he attends to a clunky red gadget belt strapped around the waistline of his emerald body suit. Then he stands to attention, reaches out his right arm and points to the portentous hazards. 'Call me Fearless,' he declaims in a rousing voice and, clicking the heels of his ruby booster-boots, Fearless Man takes flight, achieves an orbit of sorts, whips a phaser from his belt and zaps the catastrophic forebodings into a blizzard of useless confetti. A round of applause greets his safe return to earth.

'They don't make them like they used to,' an onlooker proclaims to no one in particular and, to the front, a little boy clutches his father's hand, shakes his head like a wet dog and squeals: 'Jesus, I never saw anything like that in all my life.'

Looking on, the old movie buff nods in agreement with this youthful pronouncement and, along with a cavalry of askance boys, wonders there and then what it's like to fly.

Tut tut, chides a distant voice, *take a walk down memory lane, cross the bridge between now and then, look to the harbour waters.*

And, as though taking his cue, he draws the collars of his coat, spins on his heels and strides into the night.

A captive image stays with him. I could spring her from her cell, he thinks. We could grab a souped-up car, tackle the hairpin roads, flirt dangerously together. I could even skip the small talk, he tells himself, cut to the chase.

You're a swell dish. I could go for you. Wanna see my go-fast stripes?

Through this swell of infatuation appear the hard chaws.

'Go away from me now boyos,' he tells them, 'I'm having a romantic night.'

'Pssshaw. Now we have to annoy you.'

'Three spindly stents prop the arteries to my heart. I promise you.'

'Pull the other one, granddad. It plays jingle bells.'

'Last chance, tough guys. I'll become the King of Blood.'

One of them slaps his knee. 'Do you hear that men,' he says. 'It might be a good idea to allow this one find his girl.'

Approvingly, the others yahoo and gesticulate and, like members of an abhorrent tribe, they scatter their menacing performance into the draughty throes of the drinking street. Soon after he follows.

I'll find a way to her alright, he says. To her hidden places and faraway look. I'll discover the source of those diamond lights she craves; then watch for her among the stars.

She wasn't left any choice judge, he argues. *It was him or her.*

Along the drinking street, smokers hover outside the bars. Loose topics drift skywards, half-muttered secrecies that leak through tall angular pavilions, into the black spaces thereafter where they ribbon in torrents of no consequence. Along with the unspoken wishes of the already departed. And pledges ventured to limbo, which restlessly sweep the purgatorial halls forever destined to them. Each call, rally and utterance scarcely aware of the tiny eternities they witness each night. The ghost of a long dead actress, for instance, come to haunt the personalities she could never achieve. Or the unheeded ideas, now returned to plague those long after they have dismissed any use for them. Greatness the world will never see.

By way of consolation, a lunatic street poet stands on a crate and unleashes his loathsome verse. A busker sings the voodoo blues. A girl argues her case with a forbidding boy. And in front of the long abandoned drapery a black-shawl harridan jabs at a blanket of epic bracelets with a blackthorn wand and pats her mongrel dogs.

Amidst it all, he pauses at the movie shop window. The counter-girl spots him, shakes her head, waves him inside. A screen by the entrance previews coming attractions. He passes through an ominous tone. *This is the true story of a woman and a gun and a car. The gun belonged to the woman. The car might have been yours.*

'So tell me,' the counter-girl asks him, 'did you save her tonight?'

'Some people just don't want to be saved,' he replies.

'You should stay awake for the end some time. You might be pleasantly surprised.'

'A pleasant surprise belongs to fairyland.'

'I think I might just have the very thing,' she says reaching for a title.

'This picture is as old as I am,' he says when she hands it to him. 'I bet you didn't know that.'

'No I didn't,' she says back to him, 'but I would guess that once upon a time you took every bit of it to heart.'

'I think that's part of my problem,' he says with a smile.

'You're in need of the wizard,' she replies.

'Probably, but tonight I'm happy with a stroll down to the sanctuary.'

He salutes gently and walks off.

'I hear the swans are in,' she calls after him but he doesn't hear.

He knows she's been set up by this celluloid conspiracy. Manipulated through and through by the barb-soul hoodlum and the powdered judge. Grinning either side of the only coin she has to spend.

Old man, don't waste my time, the judge booms. *Save your anxious breath. Simply put, she must and will be taken off the streets.*

The forsaken girl finally staggers away. There goes my beautiful lush, booms the poet and the boy stands watching guilty happy, each of her haggard high heel steps scraping the walls of his wanderlust heart. Not once does she look back and, from his mobile perch, the poet's unpitying interpretation wields through the air like an axe.

Waving her own wicked stick, the attention-seeking harridan casts herself centre stage. As though she has a future to tell. Or somebody's life to unravel. A crowd gathers round, each man, Jack and woman offering silent vespers that his number isn't up. 'I can tell what's in store by the tea-leaves,' the harridan rasps, 'in a set of cryptic cards or through the dragon's fearsome breath.' Squinting her withy eyes, she devotes herself to a cherub-faced boy, rubs her hands with glee and knowingly confides: 'Then again I could simply gaze into my crystal ball.'

And suddenly the poet comes bounding through her patch and delivers his damning verdict. *Humbug. Humbug. Life is a death trap.* Whereupon the harridan points to his hastily retreating steps and retorts, 'and as for you sir, your future is behind you.' The gathered crowd laughs and, encouraged now, the harridan offers her stick-like arms, leans back and, for all she is worth, decants an incommunicable blather into the fetching void.

He can almost taste her pleading lips. And his own last-chance gasps. *Your honour, for the love of God, she wouldn't harm a fly.*

Five more words, the judge thunders. *Tomorrow, first thing, she swings.*

On the bridge, night has smuggled in a steely fog out of which looms a waterside scaffolding like a gallows. The river passes swiftly underneath, and, further on, the vast iron tower of a powerlift bows in deference towards this thrust of precious estate and patiently awaits its morning command. Somewhere inside the skeletal construction a loose chain clashes with a scaffold pole and makes a hollow sound that carries through the mist out into the harbour waters and the blurry reaches of the Long Walk.

He can hear it as he crosses for the pier, where the boats are roped and repose in their calm lagoon. Lithe lines keep them, anxious ties, fearful, as though these resting vessels may take sudden flight into this alien night; and there, among them, a lone swan sits and watches still.

'Fly now,' he says, 'it's your only chance.'

And he can hear it by the water, from beyond the steaming bridge, the metal tube clanking in the night like a forlorn rapping on some primitive door, like a futile appeal, like a final say. He hears it fade and come again, and fade again once more, each distant chime tingling just inside him as are the whorling dewy specks.

And through this hollow clanking and gathering mist, among the lonely boats and misshapen souls gathered near, the hungry swans call. Call from their sanctuary at the water's edge where they pursue midnight congregations and wrangle with each other for a small piece of heaven.

The estuary waters surge now, black and noisy, towards the Long Walk's bleary lamps. Their consoling reflections warp in the offing and seem like a friendly visitation of some stellar league docked in this channel of foggy night. Beyond, a beacon weakly flickers.

Fly swan, he implores again. Swing for another shore. Spread your span of unflappable innocence and fade into a little piece of inextinguishable time. Join the purely proceeding. Glide with the wattled crane. Soar through the ranks of the black stork. Until you reach the places where the true emperors huddle, endlessly announcing in their icy jargons: *there's no place like home; there's no place like home; there's no place like home* …

At which point he knows she's free at last.

The Man Who Is Afraid Of Cows

My uncle Saj cannot believe I have accused him of cowardice. He is from Bangladesh and therefore very dubious. He just refuses to accept things at face value. He is also very stubborn. I suspect these qualities are linked. For example, he must go to Bangladesh to kill the cow and he has refused. He is as stubborn as a mule and asks hundreds of questions as though he knows nothing. In the yard, he has just interrupted my match, which is becoming an epic.

'Why am I a coward,' he asks me?

'Because you would not kill the cow,' I tell him. 'You had someone else do the deed. You paid him. Auntie told me all about it. It can mean only one thing. You are afraid of cows.'

He stands there and smiles in an unfortunate way and shakes his head like someone who regrets his choices. Over and back it goes. He reminds me of someone who is following the tennis ball back and forth across the net. But I know better. All this head shaking signifies that he cannot face up to his evasions. He is in denial.

'What are you talking about?' he says when at last his head settles back into a resting position. He still has the unfortunate smile.

'Uncle Saj,' I begin, 'because we are somehow related I will share something with you. I used to be afraid of bees. But I learned to conquer my fear.'

'How did you conquer your fear?' he asks and my radar alertness pings that he is steering our discussion in a different direction. Nevertheless, I oblige him with an answer.

'The queen of bees flew into our kitchen,' I tell him. 'I was refusing any contact with bees having experienced a trauma when the stinging ginger bee landed on my arm. The queen of bees hovered by the window. She couldn't seem to find her way. Without thinking, I slid back the patio door and guided the queen outside. She had her freedom. I had conquered my fear.'

'Bees are smaller than cows,' says my uncle. 'Who ever heard of someone being afraid of bees? You are silly being afraid of bees.'

'Bees are the most dangerous things in this country,' I inform him. 'You should try to make a connection with a cow. A Black Angus for example. Or an Aquitaine Blonde. They have wonderful eyes. They look so sad sometimes, hidden behind those long lashes. Look out for them on the back roads.'

'They look sad because they know,' says my uncle and he leaves me to ponder this strange remark.

I remain in the yard. What could cows possibly know, I ask myself? I look to the sky to supply me with the answer. Two jumbo jets ski across the atmosphere. They each leave a trail of vapour that hangs in the air. Along with my question. Then it occurs to me that my uncle is distracting me because I have discovered his secret fear. He is trying to start a feud and I must not take the bait. So I return to the important business of my match. Today, I may yet be crowned champion. There is still time. Preparing my serve, I wonder where the jet streams end.

After dark, I hunt down my uncle. I have a proposal I wish to put to him.

'The next time you must go to Bangladesh to pay someone to kill the cow because you are afraid can I come?' I say. His answer is a question.

'Why do you want to come to Bangladesh?'

I know his answer will be a question and I'm ready.

'I can help you kill the cow,' I say.

'This is terrible. Why do you want to kill the cow?'

'It will help you conquer your fear.'

He starts to speak again and then pauses. His forehead creases and pain spreads throughout his face. As he struggles with his terror, I imagine myself in a jumbo jet.

'I am afraid that will not be possible,' he finally announces.

'And why not?' I ask.

'Because there is only one person who can come to Bangladesh.'

'And who is that?'

'Jeremiah.'

'Who is Jeremiah?'

'Jeremiah is my friend.'

'And where does he live?'

'He lives in London.'

'In London?'

'Yes. But I have not seen him since he fell in love.'

He looks very unfortunate now and his head starts shaking and some more regret leaks out of him. But this is no time for mercy.

'Is he afraid of cows like you,' I ask?

'I think I will cello tape your mouth,' he tells me.

Then Auntie arrives and demands to know what's going on.

'I've been telling uncle Saj about the cows and the bees,' I say. 'But he pays no heed. He is so stubborn. He misses Geronimo. He needs cello tape.'

'And you need to get some sleep,' she says. 'Come on.'

Upstairs, Auntie tells a great story about a man who lives in the mountains with his herd of cows. He comes down to the village every two months to buy the things he and his cows need. Then off he goes back into the mountains to tend to his herd. One night he storms into the village inn. He is out of breath. His face is scratched from thorns. Fence wire has snagged his coat and trousers. 'They're charging,' the man says. 'Every one of them. It's a stampede. I chased them but it's like trying to stop the devil's herd.' The locals think he is mad. They laugh at him and tell him to come to his senses. The next morning the village is in ruins. Cars have been trampled on. Shop windows kicked in. The feed mill ransacked. 'I told you but you wouldn't listen,' says the mountain man, who is distraught. His cows have left the mountains forever and he cannot face the lonely hills.

Auntie says good night and switches off the light. I have no idea whether the story is supposed to terrorise me or send me off to sleep. I lie there thinking about the mountain man and why his herd has become feisty. I have no answers so I go downstairs and ask Auntie to tell it to me again in case I'm missing something. But according to her that's all there is to it.

I notice my uncle sitting in the corner chair. He's smoking a big cigar through a wide grin. He looks happier than he did earlier. When I finish examining Auntie's story for loopholes, he draws the cigar from his mouth and blows out a little cloud of smoke.

'They are stampeding because they know,' he says.

'Have you thought any more about my coming to Bangladesh?' I ask.

'We will talk of it tomorrow.'.

Sleep isn't easy. I dream of jumbo jets and stubborn mules in Bangladesh. In the field, a swarm of buzzing bees pesters a defenceless herd of cows. There is only one way out. The cows take flight into the endless sky. The buzzing bees give chase but soon decide better of it. I remember I have a must win match in the morning and I sleep diligently.

It's a glorious morning. Outside, I practise my serve. Hopping the ball off the ground. Arching my back. Tossing the ball. And throwing my arm at a fixed point in space. Like I saw them do it on t.v. Boom! I hit an ace every time. My serve is unreturnable. I am sure to win the tournament before morning is out. I may even retain my title in the afternoon. All I need to do is keep practising. Boom! *Oooh I say*, announces the commentator. He's very impressed.

From the corner of my eye, I see my uncle sitting on the kitchen step.

'What are you doing there?' he asks.

'I am defending my title,' I say. 'It will take a great comeback. I'm behind by two sets and a service break in the third.'

'My goodness. Yes, you will need all your resources to get back into this match. I shouldn't distract you. Eat some chocolate if your spirits are flagging. I will check with you later to see how the comeback progresses.'

'I never know when I'm beaten,' I tell him. 'It could very well go to a deciding set.'

'Watch for drop shots,' he says going back inside as I chase down another ball, to the delight of the packed gallery.

That evening, my match is still unfinished. I'm taking a breather on the step, preserving my spirit for one last effort. I think about the exciting world and about what I will do when I retire undefeated. My mind swims when I consider the options. I'm gripped by a mood of bliss. I feel removed from everyday existence and at the same time closer to it. I look beyond the yard, into the garden. A horse chestnut tree I planted two seasons ago shows promise. The vegetable ridges are in bloom. Bees plunder from the wild flowers. Beyond, I follow the back lane that leads to the forbidden swampland. What goes on there I wonder? What is it like in Bangladesh?

The umpire calls time. My match resumes. And my uncle appears. Smiling.

'My God,' he says, 'have you not yet beaten this opponent?'

'I am a wildcard entry,' I say. 'I have come out of retirement but the seeding committee has chosen to recognise neither my previous achievements nor supreme natural talent. They have placed me in the tougher half of the draw.'

'I see. You are very young to retire. But they do seem to have it in for you. It should spur you to greatness.'

'I fear no one.'

'That will help you to win.'

'I am used to winning.'

'What will happen if you lose?'

'Losing is not an option. Have you conquered your fear of cows?'

'Oh yes, that I have worked out. I did what you suggested. I took myself out to the backward roads and watched some cows chewing the green grass. It was very relaxing. They did not seem to mind my presence. They are a very beautiful animal, as you pointed out.'

'So you have conquered your fear.'

'It seems to me that perhaps I did not want to kill the cow because I have never been afraid of them. However, I am surprised I have to tell you this. You appear to know so much.'

'The cows did not mind your presence because they know,' I say to him.

'Do not continue to be silly,' he replies, turning on his heels. 'What could cows possibly know?'

When he sees I am stuck for an answer he disappears. For a grown man, he behaves in the most peculiar way. One moment he suffers. Then he is all smiles. It must be his way of avoiding fear. I should point out this observation to him. On the other hand, perhaps I'll save my breath. Besides, I'm sure he's not listening to a word I say. He is so stubborn. He will not admit that, in the matter of his fear, I am right. This is the reason our feud continues. I cannot even remember when it started. It could very well go all the way back to an ancient rivalry between stubborn mules and cows with wonderful eyes.

Meanwhile, my match remains unfinished. It is sure to enter the record books. I don't mind as long as I emerge victorious. I must watch for drop shots.

Making Love To Lana Turner

W hen Sylvia isn't looking I make love to Lana Turner. My indiscretions occur in the sitting room, in the upstairs box-room, in the guest bedroom, in the utility room and in the cloakroom beneath the stairs. Sometimes Lana beckons me into the garden. She pouts her ransom lips, shakes out her luminous hair and, before I know it, I'm crawling indiscriminately among the tangled weeds, in search of her succulent physique. Once or twice we have ended up in the garden shed.

This morning, I'm making love in the kitchen, a place where I seem to find myself for hours on end these days. The climactic moments themselves happen at one end of the new dining table, a beech-wood six-seater plucked by Sylvia from the B&Q along the edges of our town. Only I do not refer to it as the dining table. Now that I have found a consistent use for it, I refer to it as my desk.

'Go get your own table,' Sylvia says to me when she

suddenly appears, catching me unawares.

'Shoo yourself,' I reply, 'or there'll be no dinner this evening.'

'Promises, promises,' she says and leaves me be again.

After we make love I like to share my thoughts with Lana. Particularly, in the moments after my final surrender. Lana's indifferent expression tweaks a pang of uncertainty within me, a buried needle come suddenly to life that prods my innermost concerns. Once Lana's urgent appeals have subsided, I find I cannot cope with the tentative silence hovering over us.

At first, I speak without thinking. Word for word, I regurgitate the most obvious utterances as though still reeling from my initial infatuation. What does a Hollywood legend want with a washed up timber salesman? Why do my cumbersome charms never fail to impress? Will you sign my poster? I ask, having collected myself after the wild courses of our time together. It is something I ask for every time. At this stage I am like a broken record.

Soon I become braver. 'I like your flesh,' I say to Lana. 'It quivers.' And we begin all over again.

Once, after a particularly intense bout of love making, I implored Lana to run away with me. Running away has always seemed to me a good idea. You know something, honey, she said to me after a lengthy pause. You're about as smooth as an air-crash. These are the only words she has ever spoken to me, and from the moment they were uttered, she has shown no interest in anything I have to say. Truth be told, the lady has only one thing on her mind. She is insatiable.

Nevertheless, once our pleasure time together ends, I tend to ramble on. I tell her I really liked her in *The Postman Always*

Rings Twice. Her role as a dangerous lady really turned me on, I say. Especially the ocean scene near the end when she insists on swimming out until she knows she is too tired to make it safely back to shore. Though I like running away, coming face-to-face with a little danger beforehand I feel makes escape taste that little bit sweeter. And there and then I share with Lana one of my favourite pieces of wisdom - in order to know the sea you must experience it when your feet cannot touch the sand as well as when they can. I also cite our illicit affair as a concrete example of what I am talking about. So I really identified with that scene, I tell her. You are my soul mate, I say.

I mention the poster again. Actually, it's more like a large photograph, a black and white screen shot from the movie I had pinned to my bedroom wall long before Sylvia and I took up reins together. Lana is wearing her white uniform. Her hair is kinked at the ends. Her eyebrows are pencilled in. There is not one single blemish on her skin. She's standing over her injured co-star, John Garfield, her conspiratorial look lost in the hatchings of a devil-scheme. She could kill with the look in her eyes. I can think of worse ways to die.

Eventually, as I knew would happen, I mention Sylvia. I'm worried about Sylvia, I say to Lana, cutting to the chase. I barely conceal the quiet desperation in my voice. Out of the corner of my eye, I see Lana give me one of her looks. *Wake up you sap*, it says. *Open your eyes and smell the flowers.* But her flinty words are lost on me. Is there something you know that I don't I find myself asking next.

The thing is, since I started making love to Lana, I've noticed that Sylvia has been replacing me with things. Last month it was a dishwasher. 'Don't you just love turbulent appliances,' she said to me. 'No, I do not,' I replied, but she wasn't listening. She was too busy kneeling down beside the sink, her good ear clamped to the sudsy rhythms she had just fallen for.

Nor is she confining her attentions to inanimate objects. There has been talk of an Alsatian. 'What's wrong with a poodle?' I offered and she laughed. She laughed for a good while, and it took some effort on my part to persuade her that my comment was not intended as a joke - Sylvia knows well I cannot tell a joke to save my life. Currently, she is saving up to buy a horse – she reckons she can pick one up for a couple of hundred Euros. 'I could be a lover of horses,' she says, and, for once, I think she is supplying me with too much information.

Today, it is a plant.

It arrived an hour ago, in a large octagonal pot. It's an Arizona lily, although Sylvia keeps referring to it as the Amazonian lily. Upon its arrival, she placed it on a high stool waltzed home from our local one night past. She then stood the high stool by the patio doors, directly in my line of vision. Then began a litany of compliments, a litany she adds to every time the thing catches her eye.

'At least call it by its proper name,' I say.

'I want to call it the Amazonian lily,' she replies, flicking the information card bedded into the pot's soil.

Looking at it I can't see any reason why the thing should be referred to as any kind of lily. It is nothing more than a pile of glossy leaves.

Possibly our garden's exotic nature is imposing a sultry influence upon Sylvia's choice of language. When she addresses the new addition to our household, perhaps she considers the word Amazonian more in keeping with the tropical nettles and petrified toadstools that dominate our little plot. She probably thinks the word lends itself to the garden's flourishing pond life, its immortal bracts of thistle, the swampy sounds underfoot. Whatever her reasons she ignores all my attempts to have her address it by its proper name.

'Why is it on the stool?' I ask. 'It's blocking my view.'

'The guy at the garden centre said the Amazonian lily craves light,' she replies, sticking her head into the leaves. 'Otherwise it won't flower.'

Of course I'm just being flippant. My restricted garden view aside, I have another reason for lodging my complaint. The morning is lush with promise, and I'm looking forward to an earthy rumble with Lana. By the expectant look in her eyes, Lana is in a similar mood. It's too good an opportunity to squander, I tell myself. And Lana's unspoken message is reaching me loud and clear: *Get rid of her.*

Previously, to get rid of Sylvia I purchased a Black and Decker. She had been banging on about curtains for the guest bedroom. 'I want to drill holes,' she said. So, I took myself to Woodies and picked up the latest model. It has gears and comes with a rechargeable battery. I even threw in a set of drill bits. Immediately, Sylvia disappeared upstairs and the loudly whirring sounds that ensued allowed Lana and I take our unions to hitherto unknown regions. We shared pleasant gasps, joyful shrieks and a highly varied selection of situations. Particularly pleasing to my ears was a steady procession of pleas for more. Pleas that seemed to draw from the core of the earth itself, from the farthest extremities of ecstasy, if I may be so bold. I really don't know how the table withstood it all – so typical of Sylvia to pick one that will endure. Naturally, there was only so much of this I could take – my stamina isn't quite what it used to be – and, eventually, my back gave out.

So there I was. Stretched out across the beech-wood in a useless heap. Crumpled up. I was exhausted, my back was aching and you can imagine the look upon my face when I hauled myself off the table, casually looked up and saw Sylvia standing at the kitchen door, twirling the Black and Decker around her middle finger - just like a Wild West gunslinger. In the background I could hear Lana sniggering.

'This thing doesn't work,' Sylvia said.

'It makes enough noise,' I replied, and bounded across to her before she made any sudden moves.

Immediately I noticed that she had it in reverse gear. And when I politely pointed this out, so relieved was she to be able to start drilling holes again she forgot all about any suspicions my dishevelled appearance merited.

To head-off future suspicion I invented chores that involve time in the kitchen. In between bouts of love making, I now cook, scrub floor tiles, and make pot-loads of tea.

'Take the plant for a walk,' I suggest on this occasion. 'It's a beautiful day.'

'Oh I see what you're up to,' Sylvia replies. 'You are clever.'

Instead she starts dancing. She doesn't even turn on the stereo for company. Not that she needs it. She has a natural rhythm, and she moves across the spotless kitchen tiles with a wonder that makes it seem she is experiencing pleasure for the very first time. I watch her, and, for the few minutes her dance lasts, find myself in envy of her easy motion, the faraway place she locates to, her virgin joy. Momentarily, she has stepped out of the world. She is at a remove from its cold consistencies. She is aloof.

'Dance with me,' I say to her.

'Oh, you're much too busy,' she answers, concluding her intricate movement. 'Besides, you're too fond of that chair.'

She lifts the lily plant off the high stool, slides back the patio doors and steps into the garden. Through the open door, I look on as she fetches a watering can from the utility, fills it from the outside tap and directs it towards the pot.

'Moisten but do not soak,' she calls in to me through the open door. 'That's what the guy at the garden centre said.'

'I like watching you dance,' I say.

'You should see me on a horse,' she replies, maintaining her attention on the plant. 'I hope I can get it to flower. The guy told me it came all the way from Columbia. He said it can be a boy and a girl at the same time. Now stop letting me be a distraction. You have chores to attend to and I must bathe my foliage – the guy said it helps control mites.'

To look busy I take a trip as far as the kettle. On the breakfast bar I notice a photograph of Frisky – the pony Sylvia says she intends to buy. At first, it was music to my ears when she took up horse riding. Every Tuesday night she goes. She dithered for a long time before deciding it a worthwhile hobby – she considered herself a little long in the tooth for such an adventurous pursuit - but I think my unusual enthusiasm won her over. 'It's a marvellous opportunity,' I said to her. 'In time to come you can say, *before I died I learned how to ride a horse.*'

For the hour and a half she goes horse-riding I waste no time. In every room I make quick economic love to Lana. The further around the house I travel the more my back protests. But Lana doesn't want to know. I oblige as best I can, and, somehow, by the time Sylvia returns from her horses I'm sitting innocently at my desk again, waiting for her to arrive home and tell me all about it.

'Why the long face?' I say to her when she returns.

'Oh, you've made a horse joke,' she replies. 'I even get it. But you should meet these horses. Tonight, they put me on Buddy. I like Buddy. Carlos is insane. He howls at the Moon. He nearly threw me. But Buddy really knows how to go. Unlike Dude. He wouldn't budge when I tried to canter. They should have named him Dud. You should see the black stallion. Guinness they call him. He's huge. The Moon is so bright we can trot over the hills. Can you think of a better way to spend an autumn night?'

'Yes I can,' I murmur, but she is too busy talking about the pony called Frisky to take any more heed of what I have to say.

When she considers her foliage sufficiently bathed, she swaps her sandals for a pair of Wellingtons, takes up the plant again and wades into the garden. In turn, she introduces the lily to flailing limbs of bramble, to the everlasting thorn bush growing beside the shed, to clusters of dandelion spreading across the back wall.

'You forgot the toadstools,' I call out, sitting back at the table with my pot of tea.

'You're smart. You'll go far if you ever leave that chair. The guy said the flower will be the colour of blood. He said wait until you see it. I can't wait. Mulch abundantly, he said. Bait the slugs. And no direct sunlight. You should have heard him - he was very adamant. You're right though. These leaves *are* glossy.'

Just then, Lana gives me a look. *Enough talking,* it says. *Show me what you've got.* I trace my finger along her pencil-line eyebrows, my lips go to favourite places. Dutifully, Lana arranges herself across my desk, but my love-making is unsatisfactory. I am distracted, clumsy and rushed. The pain in my back soon returns me to my chair. One look from Lana says it all. *You're a klutz.*

'Don't give me that crazy stare,' I tell her.

'Who are you talking to?' Sylvia shouts into me, and I fumble my way through an unconvincing answer.

Splashing through the garden she scalps dandelions. Trims nettles. Digs up the everlasting thorn bush and moves it to another corner. She mulches her plant, pokes through its leaves, as though something integral to it is hiding from her.

She shoots a weed with a pellet gun. Digs out loose rocks. Bombs the little ponds. She pits two spiders opposite each other upon a dock leaf and waits to see what happens. Once more, she examines her plant.

'I don't understand,' she says. 'I've abundantly mulched. Baited slugs. Moistened but not soaked. I've checked the temperature. Regulated sunlight. My foliage is totally mite-free. What am I not doing? Why is the flower hiding from me?'

'Maybe it's a rebellious lily,' I offer. 'Maybe it has demands you're not meeting.'

'You're silly. How can flowers make demands?'

She kicks off her Wellingtons and steps back into the kitchen. She dances some more. Again there is no music, but she moves with ease. For a few minutes she is lost, answering her own question about hidden things, perhaps. She tiptoes across the tiles, balanced like a jewel on a wisp. She pirouettes. Then flings her spindly form into the spaces she can find.

'Where did you learn to move like that?' I ask.

'I just follow my lead,' she replies, when her feet touch the ground again. 'As for you,' she continues. 'You really need to get out of that chair. Look at you. You're like an old fish. If you stay in that chair any longer you'll go off.'

'Sylvia,' I plead mildly. 'Everything I want is right here.'

'Oh, you are a charmer. I really don't deserve you. No wonder Phyllis Kelly next door throws her eyes this way. But I really think you should step out more. You'd be amazed who you'd bump into. Last Wednesday Phyllis told me she and her Zimmer frame crashed straight into - OH MY GOD! THE AMAZONIAN LILY!'

From the comforts of my chair I take in the latest addition to our household. Through the glossy leaves emerges a solitary flower, blood-red and heart-shaped, its yellow shoot reaching out tentatively for the fading light, like an emblem of burgeoning passion. Meanwhile, around the floor tiles Sylvia performs her little turns, blows kisses to her flower, smiling to herself as she goes.

'She really is losing the run of herself,' I whisper to Lana. 'Will it ever end?' I ask.

Not that anyone is listening.

My Good Lady

I think my good lady is starting to worry about me. She says that parts of my mind are unable to keep tune with the day to day rhythms of life. Recently she has taken to buying me socks with the days of the week branded onto the soles. To keep me informed, she says. Each day has a different colour. With a thick black marker she also labels the various meats I freeze for a future day. Minced beef is marked with an M; pork chops with a P; diced lamb with an L. Lest I forget what I have to eat, I'm told. Then she pinches my skin. 'Just checking,' she says when I tell her it hurts.

I think I can trace this extra concern back to the night when a neighbour rapped at our door and told me our car was sitting in the middle of the road. We live in a hilly estate and the car had rolled down our driveway and was now blocking the way. It suddenly hit me that I had forgotten to apply the handbrake after driving home that evening. God knows how long it had been sitting out there. Thankfully, no traffic was passing when it rolled down.

'That's it, you're not getting the car,' she said to me when the car was safe in our driveway once more - with its handbrake tautly sprung.

'Are we still going away for the weekend?' I asked her, trying to steer the conversation in a different direction. I knew she was looking forward to our trip to the glens. The mountain air always took her mind off the demands of her job. She had been working very hard lately. And true enough, as soon as I started on about forest trails and crystal lakes she forgot about my defective mind. Temporarily at least. But I knew my occasional lapses genuinely concerned her.

The following day I called her at work because I needed the car. 'I'll only be twenty minutes,' I pleaded. I called in to her office, collected the keys and drove as far as the Cathedral car park, which was very convenient for where I had to go. I did my message and when I got back to the car the registration plates were gone. Front and back.

'What!' she gasped as I handed over the keys. 'You're not even gone twenty minutes.'

'I told you I wouldn't be gone long,' I said to her and she frowned. 'Who would have thought it,' I continued. 'From the Cathedral car park of all places. Front and back. They were fast movers. Probably watched every move I made.'

'We'll have to get new plates for the weekend,' she said.

'I bet they're planning a heist,' I said.

'What? Who is planning a heist?'

'The guys who took the registration plates.'

'That's it. You're not getting the car.'

'I don't need it,' I said and I walked home.

When she pulled into the driveway that evening, the car was fitted with a brand new set of plates. That's the way she is. When something needs fixing it gets fixed. There is no shilly shallying about. Instant Coffee they call her at her parents' place. One time, her mother passed favourable comments to a pair of knee high boots she was admiring in a shop window. Scarcely had the boots time to bask in all the attention lavished upon them than they were whisked away right before their admirer's eyes. And by the time her mother got home, there they were, waiting for her in a tall box on the kitchen table. There were no prizes for guessing who was responsible. 'Lord save us,' choked her mother, performing chest compressions as though a calamitous deed had just taken place. With great fanfare she was encouraged to try on the boots. They fitted like a glove.

On the Friday night we packed for our trip. I packed for the weekend. She packed for a six-month cruise.

'Where do you think you're going with all that,' I said to her.

'Is that all you're bringing,' she said back.

Later, when she thought I wasn't looking, she threw more things in my backpack. While at the same time, I emptied hers.

On Saturday morning she was pouring water over the car battery cells. Recently, the cells had acquired a sinister habit of drying out which meant that it was sometimes difficult to start the car. It had happened on our last trip away and we were very lucky in that a guy in a jeep happening by had with him a set of jump leads that he used to power up the car again. It was he who had given her the tip about watering the battery. But today we were safely on our way, a four-hour drive to the far side of the country ahead of us, towards the glens and lakes and misty mountains, and, to cap it all, it looked as though the sun was going to make an appearance.

I insisted we share the driving and, after we pulled in for a tank of petrol one hour into our drive, she reluctantly let me take over.

'Give it some welly,' she said to me as I eased off the clutch.

'I'm trying,' I said, 'but nothing happens.'

Which was true. I pressed down on the accelerator as far as it would go but the car chugged along as though it was stuck in first or second gear. Then it stopped chugging. Then it stopped.

'There's something wrong with the car,' I said.

'What's wrong is that the pump that transfers petrol from your tank to your engine has broken,' said the mechanic that we managed to get a hold of. 'Is there much petrol in it?'

'We've just put a full tank in,' I said.

'We'll have to drain it out. I hope you weren't planning a long trip. It's an awkward part to fix.'

It was also an expensive part to fix.

'Maybe we should think about getting a new car,' I said later that night when we returned home, having had to cancel our weekend. But she was too tired to answer.

The following morning I woke early, decided to let her sleep on and walked the four miles into town where I bumped into my friend Mike. I hadn't seen him in a while and he suggested we go to Sunday Jazz. I sat back and enjoyed the music and happy thrum of conversation around me. It reminded me of groggy mornings from the night before in the not so distant past. When we used to meet Mike a lot more. He had so many stories from his days in London, sad and funny at the same time, but he always made us laugh the way he told them.

'How's the good lady?' he asked me and I told him about our aborted weekend.

'I don't think she's going to be in a very good mood today,' I said, 'and she has an unbearable week ahead of her at work.'

'Listen man,' said Mike with emphasis, 'that girl is worth a million dollars and she's got the receipt to prove it.'

'Don't I know it,' I replied, 'she's very good for keeping the receipts of things.'

'You should do something this evening to make up for the weekend. Hit the town. There's nothing like a bit of *cha- cha-cha* on a Sunday night.'

Mike suddenly stood out of his chair and performed a little dance move. He pinched his nose and wriggled his body. He looked like a drowning man. But I liked his idea, so I strolled down to a restaurant she really likes and booked a table for two. It's in the old part of town and inside has the feel of a cinema. There are posters of her favourite movies on the walls. The food tastes as good as it looks and there is a music bar across the road I thought that maybe we could hit afterwards.

'I have to go into work,' she announced when I rushed home to tell her.

'On a Sunday,' I said in disbelief.

'The security cameras are down,' she said.

'What if we had been the other side of the country,' I said.

'Well it's just as well we weren't now, isn't it?'

I decided to cook a meal for when she got home. I called her office and asked at what time she expected to get away. 'I should be home by eight,' she said in a heavy voice.

I opened a packet of spaghetti. I found some garlic, Tabasco, basil leaves and *Very Lazy* chillies. I cried as I cut through an onion. I chopped a carrot into luminous discs. I sprung the lid on two tins of cherry tomatoes. It all went in the pan. It looked like soup.

As it gurgled away, I set the table, dimmed the light and opened a bottle of red wine - to let it breathe. 'Something is missing,' I murmured.

She was not happy when she arrived home. I asked what was wrong.

'This job is the pits. People are no good. I feel like jumping off a mountain.'

'Have a glass of wine,' I said to her, drawing a chair. 'Dinner is served.'

'I could get used to this,' she said, wrapping spaghetti around her fork. 'What did you put in it?'

'Whatever was there,' I said.

Then she took up this business of jumping off a mountain. 'Did you know I always wanted to do a paraglide?' she said to me. She had a few other ideas as well and she wavered from one to the other as they came to her. Abseiling. River rafting. Kite surfing. She wanted to do it all. 'It must be the wine,' I said to myself.

'I know,' she said, as though she was agreeing with me, 'we could do a sky-dive.'

'From an aeroplane,' I said to her gob-smacked.

'No, from a submarine. Of course from an aeroplane.'

I didn't say a lot after that.

When she finished her spaghetti she licked the plate. It didn't need to be washed. 'I could get used to this,' she said again. 'What's for dessert?'

'Next time,' I said and poured us another glass of wine.

I always forget something.

After that, a few more things went wrong with the car. The wipers became very noisy. Parking one night, I tore the handbrake out of its groove. And a twelve year old boy took it for a spin out the back roads, but the guards got it back to us again after a mighty chase. 'I once reversed a continental lorry across a narrow bridge,' the boy later told me.

I started cooking a little more. I find it very relaxing. Coming in late from work she seems to look forward to what I serve up. After some wine she always makes me promise to do a sky-dive. And we have huge wedges of Romantica for dessert.

A lot of the time she asks to see the soles of my feet. She spot-checks to test do I know what kind of meat I've left out. And this pinching business has progressed to a persistent scratching. 'I'm just giving you a little rub,' she says when I complain. But I don't think she realises how long her nails are.

Last night in bed she mulled over her latest Visa bill. 'We need to get a shredding machine,' she said, tearing the bill into tiny pieces. 'Why?' I asked. 'Because our identities could be stolen,' she replied.

That's what she's like, my good lady, that's the sort of thing she is liable to come out with. I think I'm starting to worry about her.

The Worst Person In Ireland

t's official. Frankie is the worst person in the country. She says so herself, and the only thing she has never done is tell a lie. Sometimes she is too honest, too quick to speak her mind.

Personally, I am envious of people with an ability to speak like this. It is refreshing to the ears, and, for a time, thwarts my tendencies to conform. In Frankie's case it has landed her in a place she would rather not be. Perhaps here there is a warning for those of us tempted towards the shimmering paths of integrity: Don't ever tell the truth. These days it is confused with being of an unsound mind.

Frankie's original condition is a mystery. Nobody even knows when it first whispered its menacing presence. To maintain this unresolved atmosphere doctors in the first hospital have sworn her to secrecy. This is another thing she does. Keeps secrets. She has been keeping them since she was first told one when she was six years old. At this stage she is brimming with them. What I'd like to know is where she finds the room. All I've ever gotten out of her about that first secret is the word poison. Possibly, this was an early clue to her future.

There are other clues. But they are unsatisfactory. All they seem to do is compound the mystery. After her stint in the first hospital, for instance, it turns out her original condition is not one but two conditions. This is what the hush-hush doctors say. So by extension, she is harbouring not one but two further secrets. This must force a strain on her fragile resources. It seems unfair.

Of course Frankie has no problem with secrecy. It is a game she knows how to play. Still. She finds it a little strange doctors want her to stay quiet about certain things. It goes further. They do not want her mingling with other patients. They do not want her discussing circumstances over the telephone. They do not trust her open mind.

'What is wrong with my daughter?' Mother asks.

'Sssh,' the doctors say, and put fingers to lips.

After that they spend a lot of time out of sight. Rumour has it they are preparing questions for Frankie. They want answers before they can treat her secret conditions. Possibly they have other matters to attend.

Meantime, Frankie is unsure. She doesn't know which doctor to favour with an answer. When question time arrives she says she would prefer to be in a room with the Gestapo. Or the CIE.

'You mean the CIA,' Mother tells her.

'No. I mean the CIE. You try getting it through to one of those bus drivers that you have no idea where you are going. Just drive I tell them. But they always insist on an answer. *This is*

the last time I ask you, love. Where are you going? But it is never the
last time. I wish they would stick to their word.'

'Let's get the hell out of here,' Mother says.

'There is nothing medically wrong with you,' announces the
doctor in the next hospital.

In hospitals, it is no surprise for a patient to greet a comment
like this with unfettered displays of euphoria. So we expect the
doctor's diagnosis to be a defining moment. But Frankie is not
euphoric. She can hardly keep her eyes open. After another
opinion, she is transferred to the topmost ward.

'Who is in charge of this idea?' Mother wants to know.

'We should be grateful,' I tell Mother. 'Frankie lacks energy.
She is not ready to step back into the real world.'

By the time she has arrived at the topmost ward we have
been told to separate the conditions from the patient. Mother
looks confused but separation does not present me with a
problem. For as long as I can remember I have been making lists
of people side by side a corresponding list of what I think is
wrong with them. It is a system I employ to detach unwary
victims from the severities of existence. My list reminds me that
foolishness and despair are not always a person's own doing.
My list is now a book.

In my book Frankie has competition. There is a set of
parents, and, not one, but two other sisters. These were the first
names to appear on my list. In time others appeared. My cousin
Tommy. The manager of the Longford branch of Dunnes Stores.
My ex-girlfriend's best friend's boyfriend. Bono. And, once he
started doing television on Friday nights, Pat Kenny. Sometimes
I remove one of the original names from the list. Once or twice, I

have added my own name.

'Are too many eggs bad for you?' Frankie wants to know when her tray of food arrives.

'The cheek of her,' Mother says, as though Frankie is not present. 'And not a word about what she's been feeding on for the last four years.'

'Get those eggs inside you,' I tell her.

'Who the hell are you giving orders to?' she now wants to know. 'And hey! Am I still on your list?'

It is difficult to break into conversation, to crack open the hard shells that have been forming around us all this time. I try not to ask questions. They don't go anywhere. Nor do I supply answers. I am afraid it will be the wrong answer, which is strange. I seldom know what I'm going to say until I've said it. Usually I regret it too. Instead, I memorise in advance what I am going to say. This helps a little. But not much. Mother asks lots of questions. They serve the same evasive function as my not-asking.

'What are the others like?' Mother asks.

'They're all nuts,' Frankie says, poking a fork through her eggs as if searching for concealed substances. 'That one over there keeps packing her suitcase. Every few minutes she is going somewhere. *Where are you going Margaret?* The nurses ask her. Then she unpacks and gets back into bed. Last week, another one took off without bothering to pack. They said she does it at the same time every year. Like a swallow flying south for winter. Now that the climate is changing they don't know when to expect her.'

'How long has she been here?'

'Don't know. Before she fled she accused everyone of sprinkling dishwashing powder into her Bolognese. There's an aftertaste, she said. A nurse told me it's the only way to get anti-depressants into her. See that one over there. Stole money from her husband's mother. She won't say how much or what she did with it. She told me she's been married for 50 years. Once for 22 years. Once for 10 years. And three times each for six years. She says her love CV reads very well. She says an acute sense of responsibility leaves her in a state of permanent unrest. That's a mouthful, isn't it? I've seen her try but she is unable to do anything for herself. They tell me I am paralysed by fear.'

'Eat those eggs,' I tell her. 'There's no point talking to us now.'

'Be quiet list-maker. I'm answering. There are three Kitties and a Katie. One of the Kitties is 88. She is not responsible. On Thursday she saw fireworks for the very first time. You should have seen her face light up. She won't let us turn on the TV. It affects her asthma. Tomorrow, she's leaving too. In a helicopter. As soon as she transfers the insurance from her car. I'll miss her but at least I'll be able to see *The Sopranos*.'

'*The Sopranos* has finished. Mother and I watch *Brothers and Sisters*. There are lots of secrets. You'd like it.'

'Please. Give me a break. Did I tell you I have a wheelchair? I am to be pushed everywhere. I'm like the Queen. You, boy. Push me. It's time for my cigarette.'

Frankie pushes aside her tray of eggs, steps out of her bed and into the chair. I wheel it to the lift. Along the corridors I test the chair for speed. The blanket sticks in the wheels and when the chair jars to a sudden standstill, Frankie is propelled headfirst to the ground. She gathers herself and steps outside for a cigarette.

Outside, it's chilly. While I pace on the spot, Mother appears with a coat for Frankie. Frankie is still answering.

'Did I tell you we have Angelina Jolie? Hello, she says. My name isn't Sharon, it's Angelina.'

'Does she look like her?'

'She looks like the Bride of Frankenstein. She has started writing her life story. She wants Helen Mirren to play her in the movie version.'

'Helen Mirren is too old to play Angelina Jolie,' Mother says.

'She's too dignified,' I say.

'She is not,' Mother blurts. 'I heard her say *Queen, my arse* on TV.'

'Be quiet now. I have to tell you both something. I woke up this morning and realised: this place is growing on me.'

'That's because it's morbid. You feel superior.'

'Yes, but I worry about people. I even worry about doctors. Especially the one who says there's nothing medically wrong with me. He pastes photographs from magazines onto cardboard rectangles. I've seen him with my own eyes. Collage for the soul he calls it.'

'Sounds like something for people who don't know how to use a crayon,' Mother says.

'The nurses are brilliant. They look out windows with me. We admire the views. There are really great views on my floor. They won't stop feeding me. They say I'm meeting targets. About these eggs…'

'Our sister is coming,' I say.

'Which one? The one who hates me or the one who wishes I was dead?'

'The one who wishes but there's no need to be like that. She just doesn't want to talk about you all the time. It's a sister-sister thing. As opposed to the brother-sister thing we have. I can separate the person from all the mysterious conditions. She just sees a nuisance. I see a nuisance and a head-case.'

'They say that's a healthier way of looking at it. Jennifer is a bitch.'

'Of course she is. She wants the whole world to go away – except her little patch.'

'She's so distant, isn't she? A distant bitch – the best place for bitches.'

'I'm going to save that for when she arrives.'

'Do. But I want credit.'

I'm glad Frankie likes it here. It *is* morbid. I wonder what my older sister will make of it all. It's unfair to call her a bitch. She is many things. But not that. Nor is she my older sister. My sisters are all younger than me. But I like to call Jennifer my older sister. It sets her apart. She has figured out her life. She is going places. Plus, she looks older than me.

Once, Jennifer told me what she really thinks. You are nothing, she said. It was towards the end of a rant – something she likes to do. You think you are something, her rant had begun. By the end of it I was nothing. We called her Six-babies when she was little. She doesn't cry as much anymore. She rants. But Six-rants doesn't have the same ring to it. She is due any moment now. I'm looking forward to her presence. I'm in the mood for a rant. I just hope she redirects it.

A man hobbles through the exit doors. He is tall, gaunt-looking, trying to grow a beard. He holds his arms out in front of him. His hands tremble. He pauses before Frankie.

'You are four great people.'

'This is The Thief,' Frankie says. 'He steals things. Cigarettes, flower vases, my pyjamas. I told him I was going to knock his block off. He said I wouldn't beat a paper bag. He said I wouldn't kick grass. He said I have less sense than tadpoles. Keep talking, I said to him. But if any more pyjamas disappear I'm going to burn your beard. Since then, he goes out of his way to pay me compliments.'

'Let's go into the grounds,' Mother says.

The grounds are pleasant. There is a pitch and putt course, a tennis court, a gazebo where patients and loved ones smoke. There are gardens with walking paths. In the distance I see deer and old men running. Frankie eyes the exit gates.

'You know what I think they should do,' she says. 'Abolish unnecessary visits. In future, circumstances must be exceptional. And once you have seen the person you came to visit, leave the hospital directly.'

'What do you think we're going to do on our way out?' I say. 'Tour the wards. Distribute cures on the QT.'

'Flowers should be banned too. The lights went out the other night. The electricians were arguing over who should change them. You should have heard them going at it. We could make a joke. How many electricians does it take to change a light bulb? The electricians are nuts. Watch out. Here's The Thief.'

'You don't have a spare cigarette,' The Thief asks a smoker passing by.

'You're exactly right I don't,' the smoker replies. 'And when I do it won't have your name on it.'

'Here you go, Thief,' Frankie says, handing him a couple of cigarettes.

'You are four great people.'

Mother often wonders how Frankie became such a warm individual. This wonder is conveyed in mantras. As a child Frankie was very distant. As a teenager Frankie was a little rip. Now that Frankie is a young adult could I kill her, Mother wonders.

Mother often asks me how I remember Frankie. Did I notice indications? There's no point asking, I always say. Besides, as soon as I could, I took off. I noticed very little. That's what your older sister says, Mother informs me.

I remember friendly terms when she was little. There was a lengthy separation after that, but I don't see it as anything to do with a lack of warmth. We both wanted to step away, and chose the first path we could take. Except for the time I told Father what she was doing with his chequebook. She cooled towards me after that. I suppose she thought it was our little secret.

'This is the nicest hospital I've been in,' she says. 'At 3a.m. last night I fell asleep. I woke up with my head inside my locker. *Are you searching for something, Frankie?* The nurse asked when she looked in. Does anybody want to see my room?'

'This place is like an art gallery,' I say en route. 'Look at those views. You can see right across the bay. There's not a cloud in the sky.'

'It's like being in a different country,' Mother says.

She has a TV in her room; books heaped onto her bedside

locker; a journal with a clasp. On the wall photographs of her dogs; swimming after a stick, drooling in her car, chasing the ocean. Don't mention the dogs, I've been warned.

'They keep you busy,' I say, pointing to her timetable for the week.

'Busy as bees,' she answers. 'We buy food and cook. We eat and talk. We look in mirrors and describe what we see. I get it wrong every time.'

'Is there anything you want?' I ask.

'A Movie. Something light.'

'I watched *Chicago* the other night,' Mother says.

'I started to watch it,' I say. 'It reminded me of Christmas. So I turned it off.'

'You're such a cynic.'

'It could be worse. I could be a sceptic.'

'I know the difference between a cynic and a septic.'

'It's sceptic, not septic.'

'Tell a cynic a compliment and he'll say *up yours too*. Tell a septic a compliment and he'll say *thanks, but I don't know that I agree*. Is Father coming?' Frankie asks then.

'Not today,' Mother replies. 'There are too many of us. Plus, I think he's coming around to the notion that I'm trying to have him killed. He accuses me of calling him back when he's halfway across a busy road. *Is there a bus coming*, he shouts over his shoulder. Actually, I do call him back but he always makes it to the other side. I don't know what he's bothered about. He'll outlive us all.'

'He told me about this policy he has. Very expensive. Guaranteed to pay out very nicely.'

'I know the one. Murder doesn't count, he warned me. So don't get any ideas. He says he has a condition for when the fateful moment arrives. If I am located within ten miles of the corpse all bets are off. Suicide doesn't count either, he said. We should humour him more.'

'Is he still obsessed with the death of Napoleon?'

'He's now convinced the English poisoned him. The English maintain it was stomach cancer. St. Helena was a desolate place. Not at all like Elba. Did you know Napoleon had an Irish doctor? His name was O'Meara.'

'Has Father told you about his dream?' Frankie asks.

'The one about the yellow frog?'

'No. The one about the red Audi. Remember he used to have a red Audi. He was emotional about it. In his dream he goes to bed convinced it is going to be stolen from his driveway. He has it every night.'

'And is it stolen?'

'I don't know. It doesn't matter. The point is that he is anxious about the future. That's what he says dreams are about. The future. Dreams are prophecies, he says. They tell you what will happen as opposed to what has. He's even come up with a way to remember them.'

'What does he want to remember an anxious future for? As if the present isn't bad enough.'

'I don't know. It doesn't matter. Every night he sets his alarm clock for six o'clock. When he wakes, he sets it again for eight o'clock. Then he goes back into a not-so-deep sleep, and at eight o'clock he remembers everything.'

'What's so special about a red Audi?' I wonder aloud.

Frankie gives me a look.

Our genes have been quarrelling for centuries. We are touchy. Feelings run deep and surface easily. It is dangerous to look directly at us. Not a good idea to tiptoe into our presence. You will regret small talk. We detect malevolent intent in this kind of thing. We have a sixth sense. We are a scary bunch when we react. If I catch somebody looking my way I imagine him meeting sinister ends. By our standards, this is a pathetic reaction. Perhaps if I was a sister or a father it would be different. We are also dogged. We survive.

My older sister arrives. She looks like she is on a mission.

'Somebody better tell *me* just exactly what the hell is going on.'

'It's always about her,' Frankie says.

'Over to you Mother,' I say, and duck into the canteen.

I order a cup of watery coffee and ten pieces of black pudding. 'Another quip like that and I'll have you barred,' the chef tells me. I receive my tray of goodies and take a seat.

Near me sits a doctor. Possibly he is a consultant specialist. Or he could be an electrician. Or a patient. It becomes more and more difficult to tell people apart. He is tucking into a plate of eggs, and wolfs them down as though his life depends on it. When he's done, a cleaner approaches his table and is quickly banished. Holding onto his knife and fork, he glares at the empty plate in front of him, as though the yellow mess now inside him has just confirmed someone's worst suspicions: Too many eggs are definitely bad for you.

Lots Of Bad Things

All the women I fall in love with head for Galway. I know this to be true because they tell me. What happens in Galway I ask myself? What is so special about the place to attract so many women? I have never been there. I must go sometime. I could look up some people I used to know.

My name is Stan. I am a baggage handler. I work at Shannon Airport - the stopover I sometimes hear them call it. I also assist when baggage goes missing. Step this way, I say to women who have lost their baggage. I then ask them for their tags and key in a search. Without exception, my search ends with the safe return of the missing bag. I am considered a wizard at my job.

When I find strayed baggage women are very grateful. When I say this I do not mean they say thank you Mr. Baggage Handler and tip me a fiver. No. I mean they are very grateful. Sometimes, when they approach me with an unhappy saga of more baggage gone missing I can tell they are telling me little lies. They just want an excuse to be grateful once again. My job can be very tiring.

Why women want to offer such gratitude is a mystery to me. I don't pull funny faces or make jokes or do unpredictable things like stand on my head and spin around quoting lines of seductive poetry. I do not have movie star good looks. No. I am small and ordinary looking. I very much like keeping to myself. I have hair problems – there is much too little on my head and a little too much on my back. I could say some more things but I hope the message is already clear: I do not have a lot going for me.

A really nice looking lady comes to me in a lot of distress. Her bag hasn't arrived. She says she feels naked without it. 'Step this way,' I say to her.

I take her tags, put in a search and, while she anxiously hangs around for an answer, I make some sympathetic conversation.

'It is an unpleasant world,' I begin. 'You have lost your bag and my wife ran away with my best friend.'

This switches her attention away from her missing bag.

'Well he's not your best friend any more, is he?' she says.

'I thought he was my friend,' I say. 'I should have known better. Friends always let each other down. At least mine do.'

'Then they are not friends,' the girl continues, and while I acknowledge her piece of useful wisdom, I take the opportunity to look at her nice looking face.

She reminds me a little of that actress Michelle Pfeiffer, only an earthier version, with her ragged hairdo and hoop-la earrings. This puts her a little older than me, but that suits me just fine. Within reason, I like mature looking women. They know a thing or two. Especially women who look like an earthy Michelle Pfeiffer.

She is thrilled when her bag arrives - it had just been placed on a different carousel. I'm disappointed I tracked it so soon, as it means my time with Michelle is drawing to a close. After she showers me with lots of earth-mother gratitude I'm not feeling all that much better.

'Where is last stop for you tonight?' I ask, trying to keep the conversation going.

'Galway,' she says. 'I'm going to Galway.'

'What's so special about Galway?' I ask.

'That's where I live,' she says, and gives me an odd look.

This parting exchange does little to lift my gloomy mood. In fact, it leaves me with an uncomfortable feeling in the pit of my stomach. The girl seemed a little put out at my query about her home town. Possibly I have hit a nerve mentioning Galway. Perhaps it is the last place on earth she wants to be tonight.

By nature I am a pessimistic person. I am always expecting the worst. For example, when I see one of those low-cost aeroplanes taking off into the turbulent sky, I do not expect it to arrive in one piece at its remote Swedish destination or whatever nonsensical airstrip it is headed for. No. At every moment, what I am waiting for is word that a blip has disappeared from the radar screen because a bargain-basement aircraft has started to break up into many pieces thirty thousand feet over the ground. To distract passengers from their likely predicament I hear stewardesses parade up and down the aisle of the shuddering aircraft selling scratch cards. 'It could be you,' they say in various languages as the aeroplane performs tail-spins. When I hear of its miraculous arrival I breathe a sigh of relief and find myself offering a surreptitious round of applause to the pilot of that aircraft. I hear the passengers do it too. So they must have been expecting the worst just like me. Not that there is time to remove the worried expression from my face - ten minutes later the aeroplane is in the sky again and the stewardesses are selling more scratch cards. 'Lighten up, Stanley,' my baggage handling colleagues say to me. But it is easier said than done. Everywhere I look I see a disaster waiting to happen.

If you haven't recently seen a disaster you haven't met my wife. When I said she ran away with my best friend I was only pretending. Nobody would be interested in running away with my wife. For starters, she isn't able to run. Any time she tries to, a mysterious fluid gathers inside her ankles, and she has to wobble like a zombie as far as her doctor to have them drained. 'Stay off your feet,' her doctor advises as he plunges his syringe and extracts a vicious looking substance that bears a close resemblance to Shiraz wine. She is very good at taking her doctor at his word.

In addition to her ankles, my wife's voice causes a lot of bother. Every time she speaks it feels as though I am being pierced through the skull with one of those very same doctor's syringes. 'This house isn't big enough for the two of us,' she shrieks if I should happen home from work just as *Grey's Anatomy*, her favourite TV show, is starting. 'Where would you like me to scatter your ashes?' she howls when I accidentally wake her from one of several naps she likes to take during her television viewing. 'Are my hands cold?' she squeals when she gets off the phone with her difficult twin sister. 'I don't want to strangle you with cold hands.' She is already doing her zombie walk towards me when she says that last bit.

It is not just by opening her mouth that my wife reveals her interest in doing me some harm. Three times a day, in fact, I detect the brunt of her intentions. So I tend to skip breakfast and lunch. Come dinner time, the trick for me seems to be to spoon my way through one of her jalapeño curries and keep my eyes from popping out of their sockets. By the time the last ladleful of curry disappears my wife's eyes don't look too good either. 'Of course I have bad eyes if I married you,' she says when I point this out during a particularly gruesome curry, and, though I am in excruciating pain myself, I laugh to make her feel good about her attempt at humour. 'Time for more surgery,' she announces, once she has licked her plate clean, and wobbles back to the television.

At this stage, I'm inclined to think that the best place for her is deep inside the undercarriage of the next cut-rate aeroplane out of here. But I know better than to suggest this. Instead, I tiptoe into the bedroom and reach under the bed for my secret bottle of milk and some tranquilisers.

Another girl has lost her bag. What is it with ladies? They are always losing their bags. I think they do it on purpose so they can go shopping for new ones. This girl is distraught. I offer her my handkerchief while I put in a search. As she dries her tears she is transformed from a snivelling bag-puss into a beauty

Lots Of Bad Things

queen. She looks a lot like that actress Uma Thurman. Only taller.

'It is an unpleasant world,' I begin. 'You have lost your bag and my wife was lost at sea.'

'Oh my God,' she gasps, returning my handkerchief.

'We were together for a long time. We were childhood sweethearts. Can I show you a photograph?'

At this point I have dipped inside my pocket for my wallet, removed a favourite photograph and pressed it into the girl's face. I can see that she is unsure how to respond.

'It's ok,' I say. 'Everybody notices the resemblance.'

'It's incredible,' the girl says.

'Put yourself in my shoes. Imagine how I feel every time *Desperate Housewives* comes on.'

At once, wave after wave of comfort flows my way, followed by a sea of gratitude - as soon as the missing bag is located. However, despite all the attention, I remain quite miserable.

'Where is last stop for you tonight?' I ask the girl.

'Oh, I'm going to hire a car and drive to Galway.'

'Galway,' I say.

'Yes. Do you know it? A man beside me on the plane couldn't say enough good things about it. It's like a mini-Venice, he said. It has a New Orleans kind of vibe.'

'Really,' I say.

'Oh yes. It's a wonderful place, he said. Anyone who's anything comes from Galway, he said. Are you from Galway?'

'No, I am not,' I say. 'Who was this man on the plane? It doesn't sound like he has seen a lot of the world, does it?'

She tells me the man is the executive of a very important

company. He has been around the world many times. New York. Bombay. Rio de Janeiro. He's seen it all.

Including wonderful Galway, I say to myself.

'Oh yes,' she says as though she has heard. 'He's seen some fine places.'

Seeing fine places holds no interest for me. Niagara Falls. Copacabana Beach. The Great Barrier Reef. What about them? So what if a book says *see The Bay of Naples and die happy*. I'd love to know what is inside the mind of whoever put that in a book. Lots of people drown in the Bay of Naples. Are they happy? Call me a pessimist if you like but that book has no clue what it is talking about. Just like the company executive who says Galway is as wonderful as Venice and New Orleans. In fact, here is some news for that man: Venice is sinking and New Orleans already has. What is *wonderful* about that? Actually, I don't know that I can bring myself to use that word. I feel queasy when I say it. I'd lay money the bottom is about to fall out of Galway. Chances are the place is already a wash-out, just like everywhere else.

Since her most recent case of swollen ankles my wife has suspended all dealings with the world. 'Everything I need to know I can get from my doctors,' she says and spends the next hour listing out the names of hospital shows she intends to watch. *To Your Health, Nip Tuck* and *Diagnosis Murder* are new favourites. In case she misses anything important she has hooked up to the television a special gadget that guarantees instant playback. And she has assembled a timber wine rack that can hold a fortnight's supply of her favourite reds. To give herself a short break from all the hospital drama, she has even slotted in an hour for watching football. I am forbidden to present myself until the game is over, and then only to acknowledge a profound observation. For example, she thinks injury time is when soccer players finally get to kick strips off each other. 'It's obvious that's all they really want to do,' she says.

She also keeps two items beside her at all times – a can of Lynx deodorant and a walking stick. From time to time, she reaches out with the can of Lynx and sprays the tulips I bought for her the day after she was laid up. 'It makes them smell nice,' she says to me. The walking-stick assists more necessary trips. It serves a dual purpose in that it allows her tap out the ground in front of her suspect eyes and provides support for her expanding ankles.

Most disturbing of all is that, like me sometimes, she has started to show an interest in pretending. 'Let's pretend we're in love,' she said a couple of nights ago - as soon as a particularly destructive episode of *Nip Tuck* had finished. 'We are in love,' I replied, thinking this a wise thing to say back. 'No we're not,' she screeched. 'We're just married. Now, get down here beside me. I want to pretend for a bit.' Sensing it would not be in my best interests to refuse, I stretched out on the sofa beside her.

In no time she became a force of nature. 'You have no idea what I'm going through,' she screamed as she tugged at my clothes and wrapped her legs around me. 'Don't just lie there,' she then screamed and sat on top of me. 'Do something,' she roared next, and before I knew what was going on she had closed her fist and caught me square on the jaw. 'Do something,' she roared again. Looking up at her reminded me why weather experts think of women when naming hurricanes. Then she closed the other fist. This is it, I thought next. This is where I check out. Afterwards, to numb the pain in my jaw, I made a bee-line for my milk and swallowed a fistful of tranquilisers. 'Are you sleeping,' I heard her say as I nodded off. 'I don't want to strangle you when you're sleeping.'

Like I say this is very disturbing. Just rubbing my swollen jaw is enough to make me think that lots of bad things are in store for me further down the line. In time to come I could well look back and say it all began with a punch. Perhaps there is a message here: begin with a bruise on your face and you are sure to lose. I didn't realise pretending could be so dangerous. Personally, I blame her current behaviour on all these hospital television shows. There are far too many doctors with deep voices patrolling the wards. Listening to them every minute of the day cannot be healthy.

A long curvy girl walks up to me. She reminds me of that actress Angelina Jolie. Only prettier. And with a better shape. I can tell she is upset about something. 'Step this way,' I say.

'Three nasty things have happened to me since I left home this morning,' she says, while we wait for her bag to be tracked. 'My purse was stolen. A detective accused me of fraud. My daughter, Lua, went to a party and hasn't come home.'

'It is an unpleasant world,' I reply. 'As a matter of fact, three nasty things have also happened to me.'

'Oh yeah,' she asks, 'which one was the worst?'

'My wife was bludgeoned and thrown into the sea,' I say.

'Was the body recovered?' she asks, after taking a moment.

'They found parts of her,' I say.

'What parts?' she asks, though I can see she doesn't really want an answer to this question.

'Her feet,' I say. 'They were inside her shoes.'

At this point the girl's mobile phone goes off. Her daughter Lua has shown up. Then the monitor in front of me starts beeping. Her missing bag has been located. Meanwhile, my spirits plummet to a new low.

'Lua,' I say, after the girl has served up a memorable smorgasbord of gratitude. 'That is a beautiful name.'

'It's Portuguese,' she says. 'It means Moon.'

'Lua,' I say again. 'If I had a daughter I think I would call her Lua.'

'Maybe you will,' she replies, fixing to leave. Then she pauses, as though remembering something important. 'Oh, I'm so sorry,' she says, bringing her hand to her mouth.

'Think nothing of it,' I say. 'Where is last stop for you tonight?'

She looks at me, as though it has only just occurred to her she has some more journeying to do.

'I haven't decided yet,' she says. 'Where would you recommend? I hear Galway's pretty cool.'

'Let me see,' I reply, ignoring the last part of her comment. 'It's a fair hike to pretty much anywhere. I suppose Cork is ok. Though you will have to travel through Limerick to get there. The Midlands are worth a look, I suppose. Though, watch out for the bog – many disappear there without trace. Whatever you do, don't go to Galway.'

'Why not?'

'Oh, you know. I hear lots of bad things happen there. Apparently, the place is riddled with dubious sorts, fortune tellers who think nothing of handing out bad news, buskers who look like Willie Nelson – and that's just for starters. Even the accountants up there are unpredictable. Some of them go around in sandals. And I hear there is a ban on trees. Imagine a city with no trees. I didn't want to mention any of this, but you talked it out of me. Don't go there. You'll be sorry.'

By the time I have finished my little speech, the girl is resting her hands on her defiant hips, a look of immense pity written across her goddess face.

'You don't get out much, do you, you poor thing?' she says, and waves bye-bye.

'Take a holiday, Stanley,' they say to me at the airport, but at this stage I don't need to say what I think of this idea. The last thing you'll see me doing at the airport is boarding an aeroplane. No. I just like watching faces come and go, wondering where-to next for them, and what plans they may have, and are they similar in any way to plans I once had.

For now, my only plan is to keep out of harm's way. However, this is proving tricky. Now that she is avoiding the world, my wife looks to me as a source of information. 'Did you meet anybody better than yourself?' she asks me when I get in from my most recent shift. She is stretched out on the sofa - a one-quarter full glass in one hand and a three-quarter empty bottle of Chianti in the other - glued to a smooth-talking surgeon's efforts to sow up a severed neck.

'Yes, I did,' I say. 'Angelina Jolie, of all people, passed through the airport. She lost her bag. It was a special gift from her husband. She was in a proper state. I sat her down, kissed her forehead and said *don't stress yourself Angelina. I will find your bag*. It was a tough search. But I found it.'

My wife gives me a stern look at the end of this.

'You kissed Angelina Jolie?' she asks.

'Yes, I did,' I say. 'On the forehead.'

The room is suddenly silent. So silent I can hear hidden pockets of dust giggling at each other.

'I suppose someone has to,' she says eventually, then rises out of the sofa, grabs her stick and can of Lynx, and takes herself into the bedroom. Following her inside, I watch as she places the can of Lynx and walking stick underneath her side of the bed, alongside my milk bottle and tranquilisers. She then climbs inside the covers. I climb in too, and make to reach for my nightly dose. But, for once, I decide to skip it. Instead, I opt to take my wife up on this pretending we're in love business and slide myself over to her, announcing into the ear I've just licked, the imminent arrival of The Big Dipper. 'I think I'm recovering,' she calls out to the darkness, as we wrestle our way through the sheets.

About the Author

ALAN MCMONAGLE was born in Sligo, grew up in Longford
and now lives in Galway.
This is his first collection of stories.

Selected Titles from Wordsonthestreet

Requiem of Love
A monologue for stage
Patricia Burke Brogan
ISBN 978-0-9552604-0-7
56 pp RRP €11.00 pb
Online Price! €9.00

Eclipsed
Patricia Burke Brogan
ISBN 978-0-9552604-4-5
100 pp RRP €11.99 pb
Online Price! €9.99

Décollage New and Selected Poems
Patricia Burke Brogan
ISBN 978-0-9552604-6-9
100 pp RRP €11.99 pb
Online Price! €9.99

The Man Who Was Haunted
By Beautiful Smells
Jarlath Fahy
ISBN 978-0-9552604-3-8
76 pp RRP €11.99
Online Price! 9.99

Log on to our online bookshop and buy at a special online price at:
www.wordsonthestreet.com

or order from:

Wordsonthestreet, Six San Antonio Park, Salthill, Galway, Ireland